A Dead Man in Istanbul

A DEAD MAN IN ISTANBUL

Michael Pearce

CARROLL & GRAF PUBLISHERS
New York

Carroll & Graf Publishers
An imprint of Avalon Publishing Group, Inc.
245 W. 17th Street
New York
NY 10011-5300
www.carrollandgraf.com

AVALON
publishing group incorporated

First published in the UK by Constable,
an imprint of Constable & Robinson Ltd 2005

First Carroll & Graf edition 2005

ISBN-13: 978-0-78671-597-8
ISBN-10: 0-7867-1597-9

Printed and bound in the EU

Chapter One

'You know Istanbul, I expect?'

'Well . . .'

'Fascinating place. Try the kebabs. There's shish and doner, of course. But lots of others. Try adana kebab. Very spicy. Especially with eyes.'

'Eyes?'

'Dead men's eyes. Sheep's eyes, really, of course. Scrumptious! Try it.'

'Yes. Yes. I will . . . Perhaps.'

About the only practical advice, actually, that they gave him. Just over a week later, in those leisurely days of 1911, he was sitting on the terrace of the British Embassy looking down on the dazzlingly blue waters of the Bosphorus, hearing the chink of ice in glasses, smelling the scent of roses and sweet peas, admiring the bougainvillea. Opposite him were Ponsonby and Rice-Cholmondely, members of the staff of the Embassy, Secretaries, he thought, although everyone here appeared to be a Secretary and none of them, as far as he could see, did any of the work that secretaries usually did. Cunningham had been a Secretary, the Second Secretary, he thought.

'So . . .?' he said encouragingly.

'Swimming the Straits. Like Leander. To get to his beloved. Only in Cunningham's case, of course, there wasn't any beloved. I think.'

'Lalagé?' suggested Rice-Cholmondely.

'I thought that was over?'

'Leila?'

'Well . . .'

'Or Felicity?'

'No, not Felicity.'

'Oh, I don't know . . . Ahmet, then?'

'It's possible, I suppose.'

'I'm sorry,' said Seymour, who was not quite getting the picture, 'are there *two* men dead?'

'Two?'

'This chap Leander . . .'

'Oh, that was some time ago. If ever.'

'Legend,' explained Rice-Cholmondely helpfully. 'Greek legend.'

'Oh.'

Down at the Mile End police station they were not strong on Greek legend.

A slightly awkward pause. Then:

'And Mr Cunningham, you say, was . . .?'

'Swimming. The Dardanelles Straits. A romantic gesture. He wanted to repeat Leander's feat.'

'And Byron's,' put in Rice-Cholmondely. 'Byron swam it, too.'

'How wide are the Straits at that point?'

'About a mile.'

'Are you sure it was . . . I mean, couldn't it have been cramp, or something?'

'Cunningham was an excellent swimmer. Captain of swimming at Harrow.'

And that was . . .? Wait a minute. A posh school.

'I see. Yes. Something else, then. Were there any boats around at the time?'

'Oh, yes. Lots. This is, after all, the Straits of the Dardanelles. The main channel between Europe and Asia. Tankers, liners, cargo ships. Boats everywhere.'

'Then mightn't he have been run down? He would have been hard to see in the water, I would have thought.'

'He had a flag.'

6

'Flag?'

'The Union Jack.'

'Even so . . .'

'In a boat. A little rowing boat.'

'Ah! So he wasn't alone?'

'Someone was rowing it, naturally.'

'Mohammed,' put in Rice-Cholmondely. 'The porter at the Embassy.'

'Surely he saw what happened?'

'My personal belief,' said Ponsonby, 'is that Mohammed is half blind. If not three-quarters.'

'He would, however . . .'

'Have seen an ocean liner? Possibly.' Ponsonby seemed doubtful.

'In any case,' said Rice-Cholmondely, 'if Cunningham had been ground under by an ocean liner, wouldn't he have been, well, mashed up?'

'And he wasn't?'

'There was only the bullet hole in the middle of his forehead.'

The Dardanelles? At least he knew where they were now. Not actually at Istanbul itself but fifty miles west along the narrow passage which ran from the Black Sea to the Mediterranean, with Europe to the north and . . . call it Turkey, to the south. The Turks wouldn't, of course. For them, at the time, it was the Ottoman Empire, which extended north of Istanbul too and they had been fighting for centuries to prove it. At the moment, however, they had been reduced to quite a small area north of Istanbul and most of what we would think of as Turkey was south of the Straits.

Put it another way, as the men at the Foreign Office had done before he left: to the north of the Straits was Europe and to the south was Asia. Istanbul was the meeting place between East and West.

And that, of course, was precisely the trouble.

'It's the old Eastern Question all over again,' the man at the Foreign Office had said.

'Eastern Question?'

'There will, of course, be war.'

'War?' said Seymour, startled. How was it he hadn't heard about this?

'Unless, somehow, we can resolve the present difficulties.'

'Unlikely,' said the older man. There had been two of them in the room, an older man and a younger one. 'With the Russians being so bloody-minded.'

'It's not them I'm worried about,' said the younger man. 'It's the Germans.'

'Well, they're not easy, either, I agree.'

'The fact is,' explained the younger man, 'the Ottoman Empire is about to collapse.'

'The sick man of Europe,' said the older man.

'If it is in Europe.'

'Sick, anyway. Indeed, about to expire.'

'So the Great Powers are, well, manoeuvring for position.'

'Queuing up to go in,' said the older man.

'Russia?' suggested Seymour supportively.

'Of course! But we can't have that, can we, old boy? Think of India!'

'Germany?'

'Can't have that, either. Think of Persia!'

'Yes. Yes, I see.'

'The fact is, old boy, we'll have to do it ourselves.'

'Do?'

'Go in. In the interests of stability.'

'What about the Turks?'

'The Turks?'

'If you're going in –'

'What's it got to do with them?'

'Well, isn't it their country –'

'But that's the whole point! If they can't look after their

own interests we have to do it for them. That's *why* we're going in.'

'Of course. Yes. I see. Of course!'

'If we are going in,' said the younger man.

'The fact is,' said the older man, 'it's all very delicately balanced.'

So delicately balanced, it soon became clear, that they didn't want someone else going in and disturbing it. Someone like Seymour.

'Do we *have* to send a policeman out?' asked the older man.

'I'm afraid so. The Prime Minister –'

'What does *he* know about it?'

'Oh, absolutely nothing. But I'm afraid it's a question of having to yield to superior force.'

'Lady C., you mean?'

'Exactly.'

'Well, of course, that does make a difference. What a pity that dammed man had to be her nephew!'

'Look, who is this Lady C.?' he had asked when he had got back to the police station.

The chief inspector had regarded him wonderingly.

'He hasn't heard of our Sybil!' he said to the sergeant.

'He's too young,' explained the sergeant. 'And too simple.'

'Shall we help him?'

'It's our duty to help the ignorant.'

'*Who* is she?' demanded Seymour.

'Take your mind back, lad, some thirty years.'

'Difficult,' said the sergeant, 'because you was just a baby in a perambulator.'

'And a gorgeous young redhead was blazing a trail through High Society. Closely and admiringly followed by the newspapers and the entire population.'

'Lady C.?'

'Just so, son.'

9

'But how –'

'The hand that rocks the cradle rocks the throne,' said the sergeant sententiously, and inaccurately.

'Is she a Royal or something?'

'"Cradle" is the key word.'

'Ah! She had a baby?'

'She didn't actually have one. Not at the time. But everyone thought she was going to. And they all thought it might be theirs.'

'Who are "they"?'

'Fast Eddie.' The then heir to the throne. 'Slippery Nick.' The present Prime Minister. 'And Lionel.'

'Lionel?'

'The Archbishop of Canterbury.'

'What, *all* of them?'

'And a few others, son. Didn't I say she blazed a trail? "Blaze", as on trees. Cut slices off. To show where you've been.'

'Hmm.'

'I think he's beginning to get the picture, sir,' said the sergeant, 'though it's a sad thing to have to spoil a young lad's innocence.'

'So this chap Cunningham would be the son –'

'Let us not go too deeply into the question of fatherhood, or the nation will fall apart. In any case, the son bit came a few years later. When she retired and got married. To a man who was just the Governor of the Bank of England, a peer of the realm, and –'

This, Seymour had to admit, was impressive form.

'No, no. Cunningham is Lady C.'s *nephew*. Or so they say. She is just his aunt. And, like any good aunt, she wants to know what happened to him. And she says that if she doesn't get to know, she'll sell her story to, oh, three or four popular newspapers. With the owners of which, as it happens, she also appears to have been on intimate terms.'

'So that's why the Foreign Office –'

'Yes, son, yes. Now you've got it. And the important

thing for you to bear in mind, as you sit idly in the Turkish sunshine, sipping a good malt and watching the blue waves lisp and crisp against the shore, is that if you get it wrong, it won't just be me who descends on you from a great height, but the whole bloody Government –'

'And the Press,' said the sergeant.

'And the Church, so don't think you can get away from it just by dying. Good luck, son! And watch your balls because the Sultan's Janissaries will have their scimitars out in a flash if you do anything naughty.'

And now here he was in Istanbul, and he *was* sipping a good malt, and he *was* watching the blue sea, although from up here on Pera Hill he couldn't exactly hear it lisp and crisp. The British Embassy was on the brow of the hill and there were other legations stretched across the summit more or less in a line, commanding a beautiful outlook over the Bosphorus. Here in the European quarter the houses were spread out and there were trees everywhere. The Embassy itself was particularly well supplied with them. On one side the grounds touched those of the new Hotel Royal, which was where he was staying. Not his choice – it was where the Embassy had put him, and he devoutly hoped that they were the ones who were going to be paying.

'A room with a view, sir?'

Well, yes. Away to the south the shimmering Sea of Marmara with the Archipelago leading into it, and, beyond, the Dardanelles forming the narrow channel to the Mediterranean. To the north, around the corner, the long stretch of the Bosphorus, teeming with steamers and cargo vessels of all kinds, and turning away in quite a different direction until it ended in the narrow entrance to the Black Sea. And then, going off at yet another tangent, was the Golden Horn, the huge harbour of Constantinople. And of Istanbul, too, which was the same place, only the Greeks called it Constantinople and the Turks called

11

it Stamboul. He was beginning to realize that this was significant.

Up here on the heights the houses were stone. Down there, in the little, dark, crowded streets by the Galata Bridge, they were wooden. On his way up to the Embassy that afternoon he had gone through them. They had been full of people: street sellers trying to sell him peanuts and roses and sweets, beggars putting out their hands for bahkshish, men in vests and skull caps lounging in the doorways, veiled, dark-gowned women in bare feet with bread ringlets round their arms, children, everywhere. He had been assailed by smells: the sweet scent of jasmine and roses, mixed with the less sweet smell of donkey dung; the more exotic smells of sandalwood and incense; and, for some reason, strongly, the smell of new leather.

The smells and the people disappeared as he climbed the hill towards the Olympian heights of the Embassy. Descend, Seymour, descend.

Which is what he did the next morning. Back down the hill, past a dismal graveyard, all dark cypresses and ruined tombs. Everywhere among the tombs there were what appeared to be milestones, only with a turban carved on top: the emblem of an entombed pasha, the cavass said. Sometimes it was surrounded by a host of little pillars: the pasha's wives and children, grouped in a kind of mortuary harem.

The cavass was a splendid figure, dressed in a close-fitting jacket covered with gold lace and with a gloved hand resting always on the richly chased dagger at his belt. More for show than for substance, Seymour judged. The cavass sat up on the box beside the driver. One of them would have done, thought Seymour, and he didn't really need the carriage either; but Ponsonby had assumed and the Embassy insisted. Lowly, Seymour might be but while he was here he was to be treated as one of the Embassy, and that meant not walking but riding, and with a cavass as escort. A cavass, he guessed, was a sort of orderly, and there were a lot of them.

Through the narrow cobbled streets at the bottom of the hill and then out on to the Galata Bridge, its boards creaking, the wooden joints heaving up and down showing the water underneath. There was a steady stream of traffic across the bridge and they joined the queue of fiacres, landaus, carts, horses and donkeys squeezing past the shapeless women and strutting effendis with their clerks holding an umbrella over their head. Then out on the other bank and down to the quays with their mixture of Western and Oriental craft, small steamers, large dhows, fishing boats and feluccas.

'A felucca, I think,' said Ponsonby, 'if we are going to visit the scene of the crime.'

Seymour, not for the first time, felt let down by antiquity. So this was the famous Hellespont? The legendary Straits of the Dardanelles, across which this chap, Leander, not to mention Cunningham, had swam? Why, it wasn't much more than a ditch. He could swim it himself.

If he had been daft enough to try. Even while he was watching, three steamers, a tanker and a warship of some sort, together with a host of Oriental sailing boats, went by. The distance wasn't the problem, nor, as far as he could see, the currents. No, the real danger was of being run down by a boat.

Especially at night. Which is when Cunningham, apparently, had swum it. Night! In the darkness! More romantic, Ponsonby had said. And, anyway, that was how it had been in the legend. Leander, a youth living at Abydos, a village on the shore, more or less where they were standing now, would swim across every night guided by Hero's lamp. Hero was a priestess at Sestos, on the other side, which was probably the reason for his going at night. It wouldn't look good to be seen going there on a regular basis, her a priestess, too!

13

No, he could see why Leander might have swum across at night. But Cunningham? There were about a billion more ships going through the Straits now than there had been then, bigger and faster. The bloke must have been off his head.

All right, he'd had a boat with him. And presumably the boat had had a lamp. But it would have been a small boat and a small lamp and an even more infinitesimal swimmer. And the chap was a responsible member of the British Embassy?

With every second, Leander was getting to seem the more reasonable man of the two.

According to Ponsonby, Cunningham had reached the shore and was just standing up when the shot was fired. He had fallen back into the water and the boatman had dragged him out on to the beach. Then he had sent at once for the kaimakam.

Kaimakam? The police? No, no, said Ponsonby, things didn't work like that in the Ottoman Empire. The police counted for nothing (that was a change, thought Seymour!). What did count was the bureaucracy. The kaimakam was the deputy of the local governor and in the Ottoman bureaucracy local governors counted for quite a lot. This one, more active than most, or, possibly, alarmed by the fact that the victim was European, had at once sent his deputy to the spot. The kaimakam had conducted an immediate investigation, although he hadn't been able to achieve much because it was dark, and had then arranged for the body to be transported back to Gelibolu, where the governor had his offices and where ice was available.

'Ice?'

'The heat,' said Ponsonby briefly.

Clearly things were different here.

Gelibolu, or Gallipoli as it was later known as, was a small

14

fishing village. Perhaps it had been larger once and perhaps that accounted for the governor having his offices there. There were the remains of a castle at one end. The small houses of the village were like blocks which had fallen from its walls, square and single storey, except for a large house in the central square, which was where the mutaserrif, as the governor was called, lived and moved and generally had his being. Two armed soldiers stood outside the front door, uniformed but in bare feet. Around the corner in a small yard other barefooted soldiers were sitting in the shade.

Inside the building the rooms were high and dark and cool. Seymour was beginning to understand now. In Istanbul you did not embrace the sun, you hid from it.

The room they were shown to contained a desk behind which a grey-haired man was sitting. He had on a dark suit and was wearing a fez, the red, pot-like hat of the Ottoman official. The two men standing beside him wore fezzes too. The man behind the desk was the mutaserrif and the worried-looking man on his left was the kaimakam. The younger man on his right appeared to be some sort of interpreter.

Ponsonby introduced him and the three men nodded gravely. Ponsonby asked if the kaimakam would explain, for Seymour's benefit, what he had found when he had got to the beach. The kaimakam cleared his throat and began to speak. He spoke in Arabic, not Turkish. After a while he stopped and the interpreter translated it into English.

By the time he had got there the beach was dark. There had been a moon but he hadn't really been able to explore the place thoroughly until the next morning when he had returned, after depositing the body. Before moving the body he had marked off its position with stones so he had no difficulty in establishing the exact spot in which it had lain. There were also the bloodstains, of course.

Cunningham Effendi appeared to have been shot just as he was standing up after completing his swim. In the

15

twilight – so it had actually been twilight not night, thought Seymour – he would have presented a clear target.

He had been able, he thought, to establish the position from which the shot had been fired. Further up the beach was an old boat and the kaimakam thought it likely that the gunman had taken cover behind that, resting the barrel of the gun on the woodwork. There were faint burn marks on the wood but, of course, they might have been caused on another occasion.

The bullet was now being examined by experts but from the size of the wound the kaimakam thought it would be found to be of small calibre. There had only been the one shot. That, and the fact that the wound had been exactly in the middle of the forehead, inclined the kaimakam to believe that the person who had fired it was an expert marksman.

There was also the obvious point that he must have known about the swim beforehand.

After firing, he had probably retreated along the beach, taking advantage of the rocks that were lying there to give him cover, and then escaped up over the cliffs. No one, it seemed, had seen him. But that, the interpreter added drily, was not unusual in Turkey.

Seymour asked if he might put a question: the beach, when he had seen it just now, appeared to be deserted. He assumed that it had been like that when Cunningham had landed. Who, then, had the boatman sent to fetch the kaimakam?

There was a little flash of acknowledgement from the interpreter and he answered without waiting for the kaimakam. No place in Anatolia, he said, was so deserted as not to have small boys around, and they had emerged as soon as the boatman had pulled Cunningham ashore. They had volunteered their services at once, offering to guard the body while Mohammed went off to seek assistance. Mohammed, who had eight small boys of his own and knew about small boys, had declined the offer and sent three of them instead to fetch the kaimakam.

Might not one of them have seen the assailant as he retreated, asked Seymour?

Again there was the acknowledging flash from the interpreter. Yes, he said, and the kaimakam had indeed made enquiries, but without result. So far, said the interpreter, a trifle grimly, implying that there might be results to come.

He had a question of his own, which again he put without previous recourse either to the mutaserrif or to the kaimakam. It related to what exactly Cunningham had been doing.

'I've told you,' said Ponsonby wearily. 'He was swimming the Straits.'

'Like Leander, yes. And Lord Byron. A romantic gesture, yes, as you have assured me. There is one difficulty in that explanation, however. Both Leander and Lord Byron swam it in the opposite direction. Which was sensible of them. Since it was on the other side that Hero was.'

'The other side?'

'Yes. According to classical legend, Leander lived at Abydos. On this side of the Straits. And swam across every night to Hero who was living at Sestos. On the *other* side of the Straits. Now, Mr Ponsonby, you have told me – repeatedly – that Mr Cunningham was a good classicist. Cambridge, I think you said? And that his imagination was fired by the classics, so much so that he wished to repeat Leander's feat. But if he was such a good classicist, and if this was so, why did he not swim in the opposite direction?'

'Who was that man?' asked Seymour, as they walked back to the felucca afterwards.

'The terjiman?'

'I thought at first he was just an interpreter.'

'Well, he is. All senior officials who come into contact with foreigners have to have one. But they're not just interpreters, they're a sort of superior private secretary, drafting correspondence, liaising with Ministries, handling anything that's political. They're the Sultan's man-on-the-spot. They assist the mutaserrif but in a way they also tell him what to do. Give him advice, at any rate. You can think of them as a sort of local Director of Political Affairs.'

'I thought he was too bright to be just an interpreter.'

'Oh, Mukhtar is bright enough.'

'He had, of course, a point,' said Seymour, trying not to sound too accusing.

Ponsonby did not reply for a moment or two. Then:

'Look,' he said. 'I know it sounds odd. I know there are problems with it. But that's what he told me. Cunningham himself. Not once but many times. And that's what he told everyone else.'

'This Leander story?'

'Yes. He would go on and on about it. He said that it was about the one interesting thing that had ever happened in Istanbul. "But it didn't happen in Istanbul!" I said. "It happened fifty miles away." "Don't be pedantic, Ponsonby," he said. "It's the curse of scholarship. What's fifty miles between friends? As long as you're not swimming it."'

'His interest was a scholarly one?'

'I wouldn't say that,' said Ponsonby doubtfully. 'More, I would say, a disputative one. You see, we have these dinners at the Embassy, when the Old Man likes us all to be there. You know, like an Officers' Mess Night. Well, of course, we've been doing it for years and we've said pretty well everything there is to say. So conversation is often, well, not as sparkling as it might be. And Cunningham got fed up. So he used to start arguments.'

'And this was one of the arguments?'

'Yes. He said that Leander's was a celebrated feat and why weren't we doing something, as an Embassy, to celebrate it? Because, as an Embassy, retorted the Old Man, it's not our job. There I disagree with you, sir, said Cunningham, and that was where the argument started.

18

'The trouble was, he wouldn't leave it. He returned to it at the next dinner. And the next. "Shut up, Cunningham," we said. "This is getting to be as boring as our other conversations." Well, this hurt him. You could see he was thinking it over, and I said, "Hello, this spells trouble." And it did.

'"It is boring," he said, "because we don't translate it into action." What sort of action, we wanted to know? "Swimming across the Straits," he said. Well, *you* can do that if you want to, we said, but . . .

'We thought that would be the end of it but the idea seemed to take hold of him. He went round telling us how he was going to do it. How *we* were going to do it. "No, we're not!" we said. He got annoyed and said we were faint-hearted and feeble. Just sane, said the Old Man, and he forbade us to do it. Not Cunningham, but the rest of us. "How would it look back at the Foreign Office if I said I'd lost all my staff attempting to swim the Dardanelles?" "You could come with us, sir," said Cunningham. "Then if it went wrong, you wouldn't have to report it." "Thank you very much, Cunningham," said the Old Man. "Why don't you try swimming the Atlantic next time?"

'Well, he couldn't seem to let it go. He would go on and on about it. He pestered everyone to at least row the boat across for him, but we all refused. Even Jarman, who had rowed in the Oxford–Cambridge Boat Race. "It's lunacy," he said. So in the end Cunningham had to get Mohammed to do it. Which was probably even greater lunacy.'

Chapter Two

There was, in fact, to be an Embassy dinner that evening.

'You are, of course, invited,' said Ponsonby. 'It will give you a chance to get to know people.'

'Thank you,' said Seymour. 'I look forward to it.'

'I wouldn't look forward too much,' said Ponsonby. 'It's nothing very special.'

'Anything I should know?'

'I don't think so. It's pretty ordinary. Black tie, of course.'

'Black tie?'

'Your man not put it in?'

'Well . . .'

'I expect you left in a bit of a hurry. Don't worry! Been in the same situation myself. We'll fix you up with something.'

He studied Seymour critically.

'Tell you what,' he said. 'You're about the same size as Cunningham. He won't be needing his now. You don't mind, do you? Wearing his clothes?'

'Well, no . . .'

'Come along, then.'

They went to Cunningham's room. Cunningham had not one but two dinner suits. Seymour tried one on.

'Perfect,' said Ponsonby. 'Now let's have a look for a shirt and tie.'

That was more difficult. Seymour's neck was thicker than Cunningham's.

'Hold on!' said Ponsonby, and dashed off. He returned with a dress shirt.

'Jarman's,' he said. 'He's got a spare. This will do for you.'

He left Seymour to do his dressing. Seymour used the opportunity to go over the room. There was nothing of much interest in it. In fact, everything was curiously impersonal, as if Cunningham had lived his life largely out of it. One thing was obvious, however: Cunningham had had money. The shoes alone would have taken care of Seymour's salary for a year.

There was little, though, of personal interest: a few knick-knacks, some invitations, a family photograph or two. Stuffed away in a drawer, as if it didn't count, was a large, carefully posed – all suits and moustaches – team photograph of the Embassy staff. There were Ponsonby and Rice-Cholmondely and this, he supposed, was the Old Man himself, sitting in the centre.

Which was Cunningham, he wondered? He turned the photograph over and looked at the back, where the names were carefully written in copperplate.

So this was Cunningham: a tall, slim figure in the back row, with fair hair and strikingly good looks. If his aunt had looked like that even Seymour could understand her cutting a swathe through Society. But something else, too: a slightly detached, sceptical look, as if all this – the posing, the photograph, the suggestion of team spirit – was in some way beneath him, as if he was lending himself for the moment to something he had no sympathy with or much interest in.

The dinner was all that Seymour disliked: everyone dressed up, flunkeys at every elbow ('Can I recommend the mint sauce, sir?'), cut glass on the polished table, arcane ritual ('The other way, I think, old chap,' as he passed the port), banal conversation – he could understand Cunningham rising in rebellion.

21

Sitting there in Cunningham's dress suit, he felt increasingly out of place. The clothes fitted in but not him. Listening to the conversation, the shared references (they all seemed to have been at school with one another, gone to the same universities, known the same people), he felt very much out of it.

At one point he overheard a conversation that, he was pretty sure, was about him.

'. . . Leander . . . Didn't know . . .'

'Didn't know?'

'Never heard of him.'

'Not a classicist, then.'

'Clearly.'

Slight pause.

'Cambridge?'

'Afraid not.'

'Well, Oxford . . .'

'Not even Oxford.'

'Surely not . . . London?'

'I don't think he went to university at all.'

'Really? Educated privately?'

'He's a policeman.'

'Good Lord! What's he doing here?'

A good question, thought Seymour.

After dinner they went out on to the terrace to take their coffee. The scent of jasmine was heavy in the air. Far away below them the Bosphorus sparkled in the moonlight.

Rice-Cholmondely was sitting next to him. Seymour had chosen to sit there because Rice-Cholmondely had seemed to be asleep and Seymour could do with less conversation. Suddenly, however, Rice-Cholmondely stirred.

'Damned shame about Cunningham,' he said.

Seymour murmured sympathetically.

'We'll miss him.'

'I'm sure, yes.'

'Used to bat No. 3. In the Embassy side. We don't play

often, of course. Mostly against the Australians. But they're good, and without Cunningham we could be in trouble. You could always count on him for a few runs.'

'Hmm. Yes. Really?'

'You don't play, yourself, by any chance?'

'Not much,' said Seymour, which was overstating it heavily.

'Pity.'

He lapsed back into silence.

Seymour was thinking about going to bed when suddenly Rice-Cholmondely stirred again.

'Why don't we go to the theatre?' he said.

'Theatre?' Seymour glanced at his watch. 'Isn't it a bit late for that?'

'Not at all, old boy. They start late out here. Cunningham and I always used to go down after an evening like this. To restore balance. That's what Cunningham used to say. Lalagé especially.'

Lalagé? Wasn't that one of the names that Ponsonby had mentioned?

'Seems a good idea,' he said.

They took the Embassy landau down to the Galata Bridge, where they left it, with strict instructions to the driver to await their return.

Unexpectedly the driver demurred.

'All on my own?' he said.

'Of course on your own!' said Rice-Cholmondely. 'Do you expect me to hold your hand? What the hell's wrong with you?'

'It's night,' said the driver, and nodded his head significantly.

'I know it's night. What's the matter with you, Ibrahim? It's never bothered you before.'

'They come out at night,' said the driver reluctantly.

'What the hell's the matter with you? Who come out at night?'

23

The driver looked around him.

'The Carneficers,' he whispered. 'The Fleshmakers.'

'Bollocks!'

'It's true!' the driver insisted. 'People have seen them.'

'Nonsense!'

'And found the bodies.'

'What absolute tripe!' said Rice-Cholmondely. 'A man like you, Ibrahim, believing such rubbish!'

Ibrahim shuffled uneasily but stuck to his guns.

'People talk, Effendi. And the story gets around.'

'It's just a story, Ibrahim. The Fleshmakers have been dead a hundred years. At least. Two hundred, three hundred.'

'People say they're back.'

'For Christ's sake! Ibrahim, there are no Fleshmakers! They've been dead a long time. Have *you* ever seen a Fleshmaker? No, and neither have I. And that's not surprising because there aren't any.'

'People have seen the bodies.'

'Look, there are always bodies around in Istanbul. What makes you think the Fleshmakers have anything to do with it?'

The driver studied his feet.

'Ibrahim, let's have some sense, please.'

'Bowstrings,' muttered the driver.

'Bowstrings? For Christ's sake, anybody can use a bowstring.'

'There aren't any bowstrings today,' muttered Ibrahim.

'Well, then –'

'But people have been strangled by bowstrings. That means they've come back. In the Sultan's hour of need.'

'The Sultan's hour of need? What rubbish! The Sultan's not in need. And if he was, he wouldn't be summoning back the Fleshmakers. Because they're dead, Ibrahim, dead! And they've been dead for a long time.'

'Perhaps it's their ghosts,' said Ibrahim. 'Perhaps it's their ghosts that have come back.'

'Ibrahim, I'm surprised at you. You, a sensible, mature

man! A driver to the British Embassy! Entertaining such ideas as this!'

'They come out at night, Effendi,' insisted the driver doggedly. 'That's why no one sees them. And why I don't like being left on my own.'

'Why the hell, Ibrahim, would a Fleshmaker – if there were Fleshmakers – pick on you?'

'Because of you, Effendi,' said the driver unexpectedly.

'Me?'

'It would be because I serve you. A foreigner and infidel. An enemy of the Sultan!'

'I am *not* an enemy of the Sultan!'

'I know you're not, Effendi, but do the Fleshmakers?'

'Look, Ibrahim, I can't waste any more time standing here arguing with you. I expect the landau to be here when I come back and I expect you to be standing beside it. If you don't like waiting on your own, then I suggest you go into that coffee house over there. And if I don't find you here when I get back, it won't be the Fleshmakers who are kicking you up the backside, it will be me!'

'Who, or what, are the Carneficers?' asked Seymour, as they walked away.

'Not are, but *were*,' corrected Rice-Cholmondely. 'Servants of the Sultan. The ones who used to do his dirty work. The Sultan's Fleshmakers.'

Rice-Cholmondely led him through a bewildering maze of dark, narrow streets where men sat outside their doors smoking bubble pipes, past coffee houses, dozens, whose owners marked out their property by driving into the ground in front of it a stout stake on top of which they placed a glass lantern containing a flaming circle of candles; past a public garden where people were sipping sherbet and listening to some Armenian singers on a bandstand; past an open-fronted building where brawny men were playing drums ('The Fire Brigade, old boy'); and finally to what appeared to be a large wooden shed.

'Here we are!' said Rice-Cholmondely, with satisfaction.

'The theatre?'

'That's right.'

He seemed about to go in.

'Won't the performance have started?'

'It's not quite like that, old boy.'

And, indeed, it wasn't. For one thing, the performance came in a kind of continuous strip; short, bloody, one-act melodramas alternated with operettas or maybe it was just one opera with a lot of acts, it was hard to tell. These were interspersed with acrobatic turns of various kinds and short comic sketches. At one point a bear was led across the stage. Hit by a cascade of peanut shells, it stopped, turned and advanced towards the front of the stage. The small boys sitting on the ground in front of the stalls scattered excitedly.

Rice-Cholmondely seized the opportunity provided by the diversion – the bear was soon hauled back – to push his way through to a box. Most of the audience was sitting on benches but at the back was a row of open, raised boxes with comfortable cane chairs and little tables beside them for drinks. The drinks were obviously an important feature and at intervals through the performance a waiter would lean over the side of a box and you would hear a noisy glug-glug-glug, which didn't, however, put the performers off, probably because the audience was making so much noise anyway. It largely ignored what was happening onstage and concentrated on chatting to neighbours and buying the peanuts wrapped in small cones of old newspaper offered by a continuous belt of small boys.

Suddenly, however, the chatter stopped. A different group of actors had come on to the stage. They began performing what Seymour gradually realized was a satirical skit. The targets appeared to be portly effendis, whom Seymour eventually, some time after the rest of the audience, perceived to be Ottoman officials of some sort, and lah-di-dah courtiers. The satire became more pointed, with the officials taking backhanders and the courtiers all too realistically backside-licking.

The targets shifted and became foreigners: daft tourists and then some very superior officials of some sort. Embassy officials, he suddenly realized. The audience began laughing and turning towards them.

'That's me, old chap,' said Rice-Cholmondely, chuckling.

And, yes, he could see that it was, a rather good take-off, in fact. And then there was someone else, also from the Embassy, presumably, but, of course, Seymour didn't know the staff well enough to tell who it was. The audience began turning again.

'And that's you,' said Rice-Cholmondely.

The target shifted once more. The actors turned soldiers and marched round the stage with sticks over their shoulders. Then they pointed them at each other and, one after another, fell down dead. The last one stood for a moment looking around him, affecting puzzlement. He took up his gun and gaped at it, surprised. Then he sat on it, propping himself up as on an umpire's stick, and shot himself up the backside, to great cheers.

The troupe went off.

'What was all that about?' said Seymour.

A short, slim figure, still in greasepaint, came into the box.

'Lalagé!' cried Rice-Cholmondely. 'You were marvellous, darling!'

'Thanks!' said Lalagé, sitting down. 'Could I have a drink, please?'

'Of course!'

Rice-Cholmondely beckoned to one of the waiters and a moment later a glass of something brightly coloured (crème de menthe?) was placed on the table at her side.

'Weren't they terr-eeble tonight?' she demanded. She

sounded French but wasn't quite. From somewhere-around-the-Mediterranean, Seymour guessed. 'Couldn't get a response out of them.'

'Oh, I don't know,' said Rice-Cholmondely. 'I thought you conjured something.'

'Had to work hard for it.' She turned to Seymour. 'Didn't you think they were a bit wooden?'

'This is Seymour,' introduced Rice-Cholmondely.

'Yes, I know. The man who's come out to find out about Cunningham.'

Seymour hoped his jaw hadn't dropped too obviously.

'You're well informed,' he said.

She shrugged.

'Have to be, in our line of business. That's where Cunningham was so helpful to us.'

'He supplied you with information?'

'Of course, it worked both ways. We supplied him, too.'

'Very helpfully,' said Rice-Cholmondely. 'Especially on the Palace.'

She shrugged again.

'We know he used us,' she said.

'How?' asked Seymour.

'He used to plant things. If he wanted to influence opinion.' She glanced at Seymour and then at Rice-Cholmondely. 'Does he know about us?'

'He's learning.'

She faced Seymour.

'You might not think it, but we're quite well known. Not many other places do stuff like ours so what we do gets around. The newspapers pick it up, the cabarets do, and one or two other theatres. We're quite famous, actually.'

'Deservedly,' said Rice-Cholmondely enthusiastically.

'And in a way it was Cunningham who did that. He came to us with some material one day and said, "Why don't you use this?" We took one look at it and said, "No, thanks." It was political, you see, and we didn't touch that

28

sort of thing. Too dangerous. "Oh, go on," he said. "It will start people talking."

'Too bloody true. And the first people who started talking were the police. They were round in a flash. Rudi managed to bribe them but he said, "No more of that, my dears." But then he found people actually missed it so we sort of slid it back in again. "There you are, darlings," Cunningham said. "Made your fortune for you."

'Well, not for us. For Rudi, more like. But I didn't like it. I began to have a funny feeling round the back of my neck. "Anyway," I said, "that sort of stuff is cabaret. We're theatre." "Cabaret *is* theatre," he said. "Maybe," I said, "but it's low theatre." "Darling, I hate to tell you this," he said, "but, as theatre goes, you are not, I'm afraid, very high." Well, it was rude of him but he did have a point. And it was nice to feel a bit established and not to be always packing our bags and moving on.'

'What sort of stuff did he get you to put on?' asked Seymour curiously.

'That sketch about the army was one of his.'

'I didn't quite understand that,' said Seymour.

'Well, I don't understand it, either. But quite a few people seemed to. Rudi for one, and he didn't like it one bit. "I can bribe the police," he said, "but I can't bribe the army. Or, at least, not that part of it." But then the Palace said they wanted it kept in. Actually, it's my belief that Cunningham had agreed it with them from the start.'

'What happened to the Palace sketch?' asked Rice-Cholmondely sleepily. 'I rather liked that.'

'They wanted that *out*. And Rudi wasn't going to argue because I think he was beginning to have a funny feeling around his neck, too.' She looked at Seymour. 'Cunningham wrote that piece, too.'

Seymour had been puzzling at something. He had been trying to relate her to the actors he had seen on the stage. But they had all seemed male. Seeing her now in the box

29

he realized how he had make the mistake. She was dressed as a man, for the last piece as a soldier. Close to, however, even Seymour could tell the difference.

'I'm surprised,' he said. 'I thought they didn't allow women on the stage. You know, this being a Muslim country.'

'Oh, they don't!'

'Then –'

'Rudi denies we are women. When the police come round.'

'But –'

'He puts on a great act when they try to inspect us. We're decent young men, he cries. Do they think that young men have no modesty? Just because they themselves have no modesty? Of course, the crowd – and he always makes sure there is a crowd of onlookers – loves this. "Pederasts!" they shout at the police. "Sodomites!" And, of course, only three of us are women. The others start taking down their trousers, and the police get all hot and bothered and go away until the next time.

'Of course, everybody knows. But it adds to our attraction. It gives them an extra *frisson* when they see us dressed up as men and pretending to be men. The ambiguity excites them. They're a bit like that here, you know. But then, it's nothing new. Think of Shakespeare's time – all those boy actors dressing up as girls. Boys,' she added, 'are very popular here, too.'

'Talking of boys,' said Rice-Cholmondely, 'I see that Ahmet's not here tonight.'

'I think he's with Selim.'

A waiter came up to the box and said something to her. She stood up.

'I've got to get backstage,' she said. 'I'm on again in five minutes. But it's just a short piece this time. I'm free afterwards. Would you like to come round?' she said to Seymour. 'Then you can come home with me. Cunningham always used to.'

'Seymour,' said Rice-Cholmondely, 'I think perhaps we should be getting back to our landau.'

'Tomorrow night, perhaps?' suggested Seymour. 'I'd like to talk to you about Cunningham.'

'I can think of more interesting things to talk about,' said Lalagé.

When they got back to the landau Ibrahim, of course, was nowhere to be found. Instead, there was a small boy asleep underneath the carriage. Rice-Cholmondely stirred him with his foot.

The boy leaped up.

'Effendi! I fetch. One minute!'

Rather more than one minute later Ibrahim appeared, buttoning his trousers.

'Effendi, a thousand apologies! I have been visiting my sister.'

'Oh, yes?' said Rice-Cholmondely, sceptically.

Despite the lateness of the hour, Seymour was up bright and early the next morning and presented himself at the Embassy, eager to get on with his enquiries.

The first person he wanted to talk to was the porter who had accompanied Cunningham by boat in his swim across the Dardanelles and who appeared to be, so far as Seymour could tell, the only actual eyewitness.

Here, however, he ran at once into difficulties. Arabic and Turkish were not among Seymour's languages and English, it seemed, was not one of the porter's. Seymour had thought that Ponsonby, or perhaps Rice-Cholmondely, might interpret for him. He learned, though, that there was a protocol in these things, as in most things to do with the Embassy. Interpreting was the preserve of the Chief Dragoman.

The Chief Dragoman was a short, alert, grey-haired man in a red fez and splendid gilt, Jewish, possibly, or perhaps

Syrian, or maybe Armenian, or, most probably, a mixture of all these; not obviously Turkish, anyway.

'I fix,' he said confidently.

The porter was the reverse of confident. He was an elderly turbaned Arab in a white gown and bare feet, at which he looked for most of the interview.

'This, Mohammed,' introduced the Dragoman. 'Salaam, Mohammed!' He turned to Seymour. 'I say, "Hi, Mohammed!"'

'Hi!' said Seymour.

The Dragoman said something in Arabic.

'I say, "Mohammed, what the hell you do in boat? You porter, not sailor!"'

Mohammed muttered something.

'Cunningham Effendi ask,' translated the Dragoman.

'Why did he ask Mohammed and not a proper boatman?'

'I ask.'

Mohammed shrugged.

'He not know,' said the Dragoman. 'But I know. He see Mohammed sitting on his ass and think, This lay-about do nothing, why not row boat? That right, yes, Mohammed?'

Mohammed nodded vigorously.

Seymour let it pass.

The Chief Dragoman continued happily, without waiting for Seymour.

'Now, Mohammed, you in boat, yes? With flag, yes? Where you get flag?'

Mohammed muttered something.

'He take from Embassy. Mohammed, this bad. You got permission? You got chitty? No? Effendi, this man steal Embassy property.'

Seymour decided it was time to assert himself.

'Never mind about the flag,' he said. 'Listen, Mohammed, I want you to tell me exactly what happened when Cunningham Effendi swam across. And let's get one thing clear from the start: which way did he swim?'

32

'Which way swim?' said the impressible Dragoman, astonished. 'For Christ's sake, everyone know that! You think he go for dip or something? No, Effendi, he swim across Straits. Like Milord.'

'Milord?'

'Milord Byron.'

'No, not like Lord Byron.'

'Not?'

'He swam the other way. From Sestos to Abydos. Not from Abydos to Sestos.'

'What the hell these places?'

'Maybe they're not called that now,' conceded Seymour.

'Abidé,' said Mohammed.

'Right. Thank you, Mohammed. Abidé, not Abydos. He swam across *to* Abidé. Yes?'

Mohammed nodded his head.

'Not the other way? Okay. Now tell me what happened.'

Mohammed made swimming motions.

'He swim,' said the Chief Dragoman.

'Right, yes. I've got that.'

Mohammed carried on swimming.

'Long way. Cunningham Effendi tired. Puff, puff!' said the Dragoman dramatically.

Mohammed shook his head.

'Too much drink!' said the Dragoman sternly. 'Cunningham Effendi near drown.'

Mohammed shook his head vigorously.

The Dragoman broke into a fit of gasping.

Mohammed shook his head even more vigorously.

'Swim, swim!' said the Dragoman desperately.

Mohammed nodded.

'Last bit!' said the Dragoman, straining every muscle. 'This is what I want to know about.'

'Nearly there!' The Dragoman floundered anguishedly towards the shore.

'And then?'

He struggled to his feet.

'Yes? And then?'

33

'Plop!' said the Dragoman, and fell in a heap on the ground.

'Just a minute, just a minute. Let *him* speak. Did he actually *see* this?'

Mohammed shook his head in denial.

'*Not* see?' said the Chief Dragoman disbelievingly.

Mohammed shook his head again, and then made strenuous rowing motions. He looked at Seymour, then touched him on the back. Then he made the rowing motions even more vigorously.

'Ah, I've got it! He didn't see because he was, of course, rowing backwards.'

'He row *backwards*? This man lunatic?'

'No, no . . .' Seymour demonstrated. 'That's the way you row. This way!'

Mohammed nodded.

'Then how he see where going?'

Seymour, and Mohammed, looked over their shoulders.

'Well, I buggered!' said the Chief Dragoman.

'So you weren't actually watching at the moment when Cunningham Effendi was shot?'

Mohammed shook his head. Then he touched his ears.

'Ah, you weren't looking, but you heard the shot?'

Mohammed affected to start. Then he looked round. Then he fell back with a gasp, covering his eyes.

This was dramatic but not informative. Seymour tried again.

After much pantomiming he established that Cunningham had been just emerging from the water. Standing, anyway. He had fallen down at the edge of the water. Mohammed had leaped from his boat, caught hold of him and dragged him up on to the beach; after which, it appeared from his description, he had first collapsed over him in grief and then delivered a funeral oration.

34

Chapter Three

The Ambassador was holding a letter in his hand.

'Ridiculous!' he fumed. 'Absolutely ridiculous! Are they trying to create an international incident? Or are they just so stupid that they're creating one without even trying? What is H.M. Government going to say to this? Absurd! That's what they'll say, and this morning I am going round to the Porte to say it first.'

He looked at the letter again.

'Absurd!' he said angrily. 'Spying! Just what is there on the peninsula to spy on, I would like to know? It's bare rock. Bare rock and sand and a handful of villages. Fortifications? To the best of my knowledge the only fortification on the peninsula is the castle at Gelibolu and that was built by Mehmet the Conqueror in the fourteenth century and has been in ruins ever since! Fortifications? Spying? Absurd! What would he have been spying *on*? What *could* he have been spying on? There's nothing there. And yet that's what they say he was doing. When he was shot.'

'Cunningham?'

'Yes.'

'They actually admit it?'

'Admit what?'

'That they shot him.'

'No, no, they don't say anything about that. Or – wait a minute. Yes, they do. They deny that they, or any subject of the Sultan, had anything to do with it. No, no, the letter is just a formal protest. About what Cunningham was doing

35

when he was shot. "Breach of diplomatic privilege." "An unfriendly act." "Illegitimate activity." What nonsense!'

He put the letter down on his desk.

'They shoot one of my staff. And then they have the nerve to write to me and complain! They wish to lodge a formal protest, they say. Just wait till I tell H.M. Government and they'll register a protest, all right. With warships!'

He looked at the letter again, disbelievingly.

'Spying? One of my staff? Ridiculous!'

He picked the letter up and waved it under Seymour's nose.

'And they say he's done it before! That he does it repeatedly!'

'Swim the Straits?' said Seymour, surprised.

'No, no. Apparently he sails up and down scrutinizing the cliffs. And, of course, he's been using binoculars. How else is he going to see them, I'd like to know?'

'See . . .?'

'The birds.'

'Birds!'

'Shearwater. Splendid place for observing them, the Dardanelles. They congregate there. In their thousands. Not just the Dardanelles, of course; you also see them in the Bosphorus and in the Sea of Marmara. But the point about the Dardanelles is that there you can observe them in flight. And that's very interesting, Seymour, because they fly very low down, right at the surface of the water, their legs practically touching it. Fascinating! So no wonder Cunningham was studying them.'

'That's what he was doing, was he?'

'Well, of course. What else would he have been doing?'

'While he was sailing up and down?'

'Well, he wouldn't be doing it while he was swimming, would he?'

'"Up and down" suggests that he did it quite a lot.'

'Well, yes. He was probably *very* interested in them. I'm

36

very interested myself. Do you know, Seymour, that although they are pelagic birds they lay their eggs on the land? Well, I suppose they would have to, wouldn't they? I mean, they couldn't lay them on the sea. But the thing is, you see, they only lay a single egg. A white one. And they lay it underground. Isn't that remarkable?'

'Er, yes. Astonishing!'

'So of course Cunningham was looking closely. And through binoculars. It would be easy to miss, wouldn't it?'

'Well, yes.'

'But of course there would be thousands of them, so you'd stand a good chance.'

'Well, yes. Yes. I suppose so. Of course it could give rise to suspicion, couldn't it? I mean, it's not something the average Turk would understand.'

'Oh, I don't know. There are some good ornithologists among the Turks.'

'And Cunningham – was he an ornithologist?'

'I don't know about that. I don't think I'd go as far as that. A general interest, I would say. I remember talking to him once about the shearwater and he listened most attentively.'

'Oh, good. And – and he was a keen sailor?'

'Oh, I wouldn't say that, either. I think it was rather that he was keen on Felicity Singleton-Mainwaring. And she certainly is a keen sailor. I expect it was her boat.'

'Oh, Lord!' said Felicity. 'Are they really saying that? Well, it's true we have been sailing up and down there a lot recently. "Come on, Felicity: make yourself useful for once!" he said. Well, I didn't mind. I *like* sailing. And it's nice to have a bit of company. And Peter is all right as company. At least, he *can* be all right as company when he gives his mind to it.

'But it wasn't just once, it was every afternoon. "I can't," I said. "I'm playing tennis with Daphne." "No, you're

37

not," he said. "You're coming for a sail with me." Daphne was very cross. "You let him order you around like a little dog," she said. "I *like* sailing," I said. "You like tennis, too," she said. "And you promised!" But I don't think it was that, really, I think she was a teeny bit jealous. You see, she fancies Peter herself. They had a tiny bit of a fling once.

'Well, I thought I could see a brilliant way of solving everything. "Why don't you come with us in the boat?" I said to Daphne. But she flew into a temper. "Listen," she said, "I want to play tennis. We've *booked* to play tennis. And, anyway, I don't want to go sailing with that man, I don't want to go *anywhere* with that man!" And he said, "Oh, God! Not *two* of you!"

'"That's not very nice of you," I said. "After all, it's my boat." "So it is," he said, "and I can't go without it. And you, unfortunately."

'"I promised," I said. "But aren't you promised to me, too, darling Felicity, for ever and ever? At least, I thought that's what you told me one drunken evening. Well, a promise is a promise, Felicity, and you've got to stand by it. And mine was first. So you're coming with me. Now where is this bloody boat?"

'Well, I didn't mind once. But every afternoon! "I've got something better to do with my life," I said. "No, you haven't, Felicity. Not if you really think about it. And it's not every afternoon. It's every afternoon for a bit. Then you can go and play tennis with Daphne. Anyway, you're always telling me you like sailing."

'"Can't we go and sail somewhere else? The Bosphorus, for instance? I'm sure you'd like that." "No, I wouldn't," he said. "It's got to be the bleeding, boring Dardanelles. So take me in close so that I can get a better look."

'What was he looking at? Well, I don't know, I couldn't see anything there much to look at myself. Birds? *Birds*! *Are* there any birds there? I thought shearwater stayed out at sea. Birds? There were a couple of women there who were sunbathing, but . . .

38

'No, it was just up and down. And always the same side. Not the one he put me down on.

'Yes, he put me down. On the other side of the Straits. So that he could swim across to me. "You are my beacon, my lighthouse, Felicity. You are my Hero and I am going to swim across to you just as Leander did. There! Doesn't that make you feel good? Well, it ought to. You will feel yourself part of legend, my beautiful, beautiful Felicity, one of the most romantic legends in the world. You, Felicity! My beautiful Felicity. It's like Romeo and Juliet or Antony and Cleopatra, and you are half of it. Christ, what are you complaining about? Any other girl would jump at the chance. Any girl who was halfway decently romantic and didn't care more for her boat than her man –"

'"Hey!" I said. "What are you doing? That's my boat!" "I'm just borrowing it for a bit," he said. "You stand there until I get back." "But you don't know how to sail!" I said. "I'll work it out," he said. "Don't make such a fuss of things, Felicity." "But it's my boat!" "And it will be brought back to you very shortly. Christ, how do we put this bloody thing into reverse?"

'"But I thought you were going to swim? Like Leander?" "Listen, you dimwit, I *am* going to swim. I am going to swim right across the Straits to you, my Hero, who will be standing here, on the rocks, waiting for me." "Yes, but if you swim across, the boat will be on the other side, and we'll both be on this side, and then how will we get home?"

'"My beautiful, brainless Felicity, this is just a rehearsal. I'm just going to sail the boat across so that I can get an idea of what it would be like. And then I'm going to come back here, in the boat, and pick you up, and we can sail back home together; unless I change my mind and sail home by myself leaving you here frying on the rock."

'"Why can't I come with you? I could sail the boat and you could look –" "I need to think, darling. And I can't think with you prattling away. So you stay here out of

39

harm's way. Anyway, that's more realistic. This is where you'll be when we do it properly."

'"Hey!" I said. "Wait a minute –"'

But the boat had already gone.

'Yes, he did bring it back. Safely. Although he did have some trouble bringing it in. "But you are right, Felicity, about the boat and the side. I shall need two boats. At least. One to accompany me across so that one of those daft cargo vessels doesn't run me down, and one to put you there for me to swim across to."

'No, I didn't actually do it in the end. Only in the rehearsal. So that he could see it in his mind, he said. On reflection, he said, he could see there was more to it than he had thought. I was rather sorry. I'd thought myself into it and rather liked the idea of being Hero. You know, his swimming across to me. Of course I know he didn't care tuppence for me really, but all the same . . .'

They were a rum lot, thought Seymour, from the Ambassador down. Even Felicity. *Could* she be as bovine as she appeared? Well, yes, Seymour was afraid, on the basis of his brief acquaintance with her, she could. A nice, healthy girl from the shires, one of those upper-class girls who kept a pony and lived for horses and hadn't an idea in her head. But what was a nice healthy girl from the shires doing here? On her own? Without her horses? She wasn't a member of the Embassy staff, although she was known to all of them. What did she do in life?

'Felicity? Oh, she just floats around,' said Ponsonby.

But what had led her to float around in Istanbul? Cunningham? She was, Ponsonby had said, a sort of cousin of his. Had she had, as Felicity herself might have said, a teeny bit of a crush on him? Probably. But how deep had the crush been? From the way she had spoken, she seemed to lead a self-sufficient life here, independent of him; and Seymour had an uneasy suspicion that in

Felicity's mind no great distinction was made between a man and a horse.

So what was she doing here? Single women, in those days, did not normally go off and live by themselves, and certainly not alone by themselves in Istanbul.

Maybe it was different in the upper class.

And then, what about Cunningham? He was a bit of a rum one, too, even more so if anything. The way he had spoken to her! But maybe that was the way the upper class spoke to its cousins.

What the hell was a man like Cunningham doing writing scripts for a seedy theatre company? 'He was in the Footlights, old man,' said Ponsonby, as if that were sufficient explanation. Footlights? Seymour was mystified. 'Cambridge Footlights,' Ponsonby had expanded. Seymour was even more mystified.

Something to do with Cambridge University, obviously. (Everything in this Embassy seemed to have something to do with Cambridge.) And to do with the stage. But what had the Embassy to do with the theatre? A means of influencing opinion, as Lalagé had suggested? But – was that the way embassies normally went about influencing public opinion? A rum way of going on.

About one thing, though, he thought he was less mystified, and that was what Cunningham had been up to when he was sailing up and down looking at the Gelibolu cliffs: spying, despite what the Old Man had said. There could be no other explanation: could there?

But then, how did this swimming the Straits fit in? Spying from a boat, yes, he could see that; but . . . swimming? Across the Dardanelles? If you were trying to spy on the land the other side, wasn't that, well, an odd way of going about it?

Rum, he thought: decidedly rum.

And, if you were trying to spy, amateur. That was the thought that was in his mind when he returned to the

41

Embassy. It was four o'clock and they were serving tea out on the terrace. Tea. Of course, they drank tea in the police station at Whitechapel, although Seymour himself didn't. But it wasn't quite tea like this. In the police station they grabbed a mug and put it on the desk and got on with their work. Here it was a social occasion. Everyone congregated out there, among the roses. Servants went round serving it, a rather superior blend, in fragile, beautiful teacups. People chatted idly; about tennis, music, mutual acquaintances. Certainly not about politics or diplomacy or work. It was rather pleasant out there after the heat of the day, getting the first touch of the evening breeze. Relaxed. Gracious.

Not fraught and puritanical and hectic and driven, all the things that Seymour normally associated with work, but civilized, gracious. Gracious, yes: but also, he came back to it, amateur. The life of the gentleman before the Flood. Seymour, unfortunately, was part of the Flood.

It was a thought which was reinforced by an encounter he had with someone he had not seen before, a trim, erect, bushy-moustached man in a smart white suit. He was talking to Ponsonby.

'Oh, hello, Seymour,' said Ponsonby, with a certain relief. 'Can I introduce you? This is Chalmers. Our military attaché. I was just telling him about the Old Man's visit to the Porte this morning.'

Seymour knew now that 'Porte' didn't mean 'port', as with ships. But nor did it mean 'door' or 'gate', as in French for. It was Diplomatic Familiar for the Sublime Porte, which was, as far as diplomacy was concerned, the Ottoman Empire's seat of government.

'Oh, yes?' he said. 'How did it go?'

'Deuce,' said Ponsonby. 'Forty-all. We made our protest, they made theirs.'

'And what will come of it?'

'Probably nothing. Which may, of course,' said Ponsonby thoughtfully, 'suit both sides.'

'But will the people back at home be satisfied with nothing?'

Lady C. for instance.

'Probably not. But it may take a time for the game to move on.'

'If it doesn't move back,' said Chalmers. 'Damned irritating, that man Cunningham.'

'What was he up to?' asked Seymour. 'Sailing up and down the Straits with a pair of binoculars.'

'Bird-watching,' said Ponsonby. 'According to the Old Man.'

'*Was* he spying?'

'Shouldn't have been,' said Chalmers. 'That's my job.'

'Might have been, I suppose,' said Ponsonby. 'Cunningham always played his own hand.'

'He damned well shouldn't have been playing his own hand,' said Chalmers angrily. 'He's a diplomat, isn't he? Why didn't he stick to his own job? The Old Man should have jumped on him.'

'He used to, regularly,' said Ponsonby. 'But, somehow, when he landed Cunningham was never quite there.'

'The trouble with the Old Man is that he lacks authority,' complained Chalmers. 'There's no discipline in this Embassy. And you see where you get when there's no discipline. An entirely avoidable international incident!'

'Not quite yet, old boy,' said Ponsonby and drifted away.

'And that's another thing,' said Chalmers. 'These diplomats think they can fix everything with a chat. But when the differences are real, you're not always able to.' He looked at Seymour. 'You'll have guessed I'm not a diplomat.'

'A soldier, I imagine?'

'Too true. And glad of it.'

'What do you make of this Cunningham business?'

'The man was obviously spying. All this stuff about Leander and Hero! A ruse. To put people off the scent.

43

Swim across the Straits? A lunatic action if ever I heard of one. And all to get to a man!'

'Man?'

'Hero. Must be a man, mustn't it? Otherwise it would be Heroine.'

'I think it was different in those days.'

'How do you mean, it was different?'

'Well, "Hero" is, I gather, or was, a girl's name.'

'There you are! Confusing people. To put them off the scent. Just the sort of thing Cunningham would do.'

'I gather you've not got a high opinion of Cunningham.'

'Tricky. Always up to something. And usually something he shouldn't be. I'm not saying anything about the women, mind. I don't go in for that sort of thing myself, but I can understand that a single man, out here in Istanbul, well . . .! No, it's not that. It's that he should stick to his own line of business and keep clear of other people's.'

'Yours, for example?'

'Too right. Look, old man, you're a policeman, I gather? I've got a great respect for policemen. They do their job. They're professionals. Well, look, old man, a military attaché is like that. He knows about war. Professionally. And he knows a bit about spying, too. He has to. It's part of his job. He's a professional. And he doesn't need bloody amateurs creeping in and cocking things up!'

'You think that's what he was doing?'

'What else could be he doing?'

'The Old Man seemed to be pretty sure there was nothing there to be spying on.'

'Well, there isn't. At the moment.'

'At the moment? You mean –'

'Look, old boy, it's not something I can go into. You'll understand that, you're a professional yourself. Let's just say that it's come to our ears – well, my ears, actually – that the Ottomans are planning to build some fortifications over on that side of the Straits. It makes sense, if you think about it. The Dardanelles is the main link between the

Black Sea and the Bosphorus and the Mediterranean. Any big Power will want to control it. Believe me, old boy, I know! So the Turks will want to stop them controlling it. So, well, they're going to need to do something about it. Put some gun emplacements there, for a start. So the Old Man is right, yes, at the moment. But, come a few months, and he won't be. Now, it's sense to keep an eye on it, and that's what I'm doing. Discreetly. And we don't want some jumped-up Johnny sticking his oar in and drawing everyone's attention to the fact that we know about it and are keeping our eye on it!'

After Chalmers had gone, Ponsonby came back and dropped into the chair beside Seymour.

'Sorry about that,' he said. 'Leaving you landed with Chalmers. He's something to be taken in small doses. We keep sending him away to spy out the interior of Anatolia. The trouble is, he keeps coming back. Usually with another bee in his bonnet.'

'Like the Dardanelles?'

'He's been on about that, has he? Amazing man – he sees fortifications sprouting up in all sorts of unlikely places.'

'He doesn't seem to think much of Cunningham.'

'Mutual, old boy. Cunningham didn't think much of him. Reckoned he was a complete blockhead.'

'So he might have thought it necessary to supplement his efforts?'

'Spying, you mean? Well, he might. We used to suggest that sometimes just to get up Chalmers' nose. But I would have thought that was about as likely as bird-watching. You've got to understand that there's a bit of a code about that in the Diplomatic. It's the sort of thing you don't do. Except if you're a military attaché. Now, I'll admit that Cunningham was the kind of man who would do plenty of things that ordinary diplomats don't do, but . . . spying? A bit infra dig, old man, especially for someone like Cunningham.

'And there's another thing: you don't spy on your own, you do it for somebody. There's always someone you're passing the information to. But – apart from the fact that Cunningham found it difficult to work for anyone – who could that have been in Cunningham's case? Not the F.O., old boy, it doesn't go in for that sort of thing. And if it did in Istanbul, the Old Man would have to know about it. Strictly hierarchical, we are.

'The army? They're the ones who normally do intelligence work. But I've told you what Cunningham thought of Chalmers, and he thought much the same about the army. Who else, then? A private mission for the Prime Minister? I don't think so.

'No, I'd forget about spying. The only spying Cunningham would be likely to have done would have been to work out beforehand how he was going to climb up into some woman's bedroom.'

But not, surely, on the Gelibolu side of the Straits, where, from what they all said, the ground was barren, the peninsula depopulated, and likely women even fewer than the fortifications. On the other side, then, to which Leander had swum and where Cunningham had temporarily marooned Felicity? But that, too, seemed unlikely. From what Seymour had seen, the land was as barren and as empty as it was on the Gelibolu side. To emulate Leander, Cunningham had had to actually put a woman there: Felicity.

But – hold on a minute – Felicity had been there only for the rehearsal. Had there been some other woman there for the real thing?

Seymour needed to question Mohammed again. On the whole he would have preferred to have done it, despite the language difficulty, without the help of the Chief Dragoman. But there was a protocol in this, he had learned, and Seymour had gone native sufficiently as not to wish to break it. Reluctantly he went in search of the Dragoman.

'Sure!' said the Dragoman happily. 'We question Mohammed. What you want to know?'

'Was there a woman on the other side when they set out?'

'A woman! Oh, ho!' said the Chief Dragoman, rubbing his hands lubriciously.

'Mohammed, what you up to? You and Cunningham Effendi? Some nice juicy lady, yes? I surprise.'

'Me?' said Mohammed, amazed.

'You visit some lady's house, yes? Before you go in boat? Mohammed, I impressed. First, the lady, then the rowing. You strong man, Mohammed. No wonder you eight children.'

Mohammed opened his mouth, then closed it.

'And with Cunningham Effendi, too! How you do it, Mohammed? Together?'

Mohammed looked at the Chief Dragoman, then at Seymour, and moved away worried.

'Wait a minute, wait a minute! said Seymour. 'Listen, Mohammed: no juicy lady. Right?'

'No juicy lady?' said the Dragoman, disappointed.

'No. All I want to know, Mohammed, is: was there a woman with Cunningham when you went to the other side of the Straits to start?'

Mohammed's look of alarm returned.

'Woman?' he unmistakably said. And Seymour reckoned he could understand the next bit too: 'Are you crazy, or something?'

'No woman,' said the Chief Dragoman sadly.

But, then, thought Seymour, if for some reason Cunningham was doing it all in reverse, wouldn't the woman, after all, have been on the Gelibolu side? Ought he not to ask Mohammed about that?

Just at the moment, though, he felt he wouldn't.

The Chief Dragoman was deep in thought.

'Effendi,' he said, after a moment, 'what's the problem?
You want woman? I fix.'

That evening Seymour went to the theatre to see Lalagé.
Not for the reason the Chief Dragoman had supposed nor
Lalagé suggested but strictly on business. Nor did he go in
the Embassy landau. It wasn't just that sitting up there
with the driver and a gilt-edged cavass beside him he felt
rather foolish. It was more that he was increasingly beginning to feel cut off. The Embassy trappings had closed
round him like a screen, shielding him, no doubt, from
unwanted intimacies but also separating him from, well,
life. He had some sympathy with Cunningham wanting to
go down into the city after a rarefied Embassy dinner on
the heights.

And which was it that had occasioned Cunningham's
death? Life on the heights or life down below? Some
complex diplomatic reason or even doubtfully diplomatic
reason, spying, for example? Anyway something to do
with international politics? Or something more personal, a
woman, perhaps, anyway something to do with ordinary
life?

If it was the latter, he doubted whether he would find
out much from the Embassy staff. Not even from the
drivers and porters and cavasses who usually knew so
much. He had a feeling that Cunningham would simply
have left them behind, as he and Rice-Cholmondely had
done, and plunged off into the streets alone.

No, he would have to talk to someone in the streets and
the person who inevitably came to mind was Lalagé. She
seemed to have been on intimate terms with Cunningham
and might know about that side of him. And not only that.
There was obviously some intelligence-gathering relationship between the Embassy and some at least of the theatre
players, and she might be able to enlighten him about that,
too.

So he set off on foot. Down the hill, past the cemetery

with the turbaned pillars, into the narrow crowded streets with their exotic smells and noises.

Almost at once he learned why the diplomats normally made use of the carriage. It was swelteringly hot and by the time he reached the Galata Bridge his shirt was drenched with sweat. He paused for a moment by the bridge, looking down into the water and at the array of ships, and gathering his breath.

Seymour liked docks. He had spent all his life within a mile of the London docks. Even when he had been posted to the Special Branch he had continued to work in that area, where his skill at languages helped him with the immigrants who abounded there. He came from an immigrant family himself, back a little way. His grandfather had come from Poland, his mother from Hungary. They had landed in the docks and then, like so many other immigrant families, had stayed.

Seymour had grown up there among the many languages of the East End and had very early developed an ear for them. So good an ear, in fact, that the police interpreter had noticed it and began to take him round with him. This in turn had led to the police noticing him and eventually to his joining the police. He had become known as 'the languages man' and so when the Foreign Office had asked for someone with knowledge of foreign languages his name had been the one that was put forward.

But it wasn't just the languages. His upbringing had given him a sense of the people and lives behind the languages. That sense was missing here; but now, as he went about on foot, hearing the talk and seeing the people, he began to capture it a little. The Arabic and Turkish he could not understand, although he was beginning to grasp them a little. But there were other languages in the streets, too, Italian and German and French, and these he had no difficulty with. For all the differences, this part of Istanbul was not actually that different from the East End.

He found his way through to the theatre, stopping in the

park to listen to the music, turning aside for a leisurely cup of coffee in one of the candlelit coffee houses. Although it was dark now, the evening was pleasantly warm. The people were relaxed. He began to feel comfortable and at home.

He didn't want to arrive too early at the theatre. He had arranged to meet Lalagé after the performance. He would take her out for a meal in one of the restaurants nearby.

There seemed to be quite a crowd in the street outside the theatre. There were people in uniforms. There seemed to have been an accident of some sort.

A carriage was standing by the side door. It was different from the other carriages he had seen, more box-like and without seats. Some men were opening the back of the carriage. It fell down into a flap. The men reached inside and pulled out a stretcher.

A senior-looking man in a fez came out of the theatre and stood for a moment talking to the stretcher-bearers. Then he stood aside to let them go in. His eye, just at that moment, caught Seymour's.

'Why, Mr Seymour!' he said. 'What brings you here?'

It was Mukhtar, the terjiman from Gelibolu.

Seymour pushed his way through towards him.

'I was meeting someone,' he said. 'One of the actresses.'

The terjiman's eyebrows went up.

'Actresses?' he said.

'Players,' amended Seymour. He didn't want to get the theatre into trouble.

'Really?' said Mukhtar. He beckoned Seymour towards him and they went in. He led Seymour along a corridor and up some stairs.

They went into a room. A woman was lying on a bed, her head turned away.

'Not this one?' said the terjiman.

Chapter Four

'Yes,' said Seymour.

The terjiman nodded.

'I shall ask you some questions, please,' he said. 'One moment!'

The stretcher-bearers came in. They looked at the terjiman enquiringly. He made a gesture of assent and they lifted the body on to the stretcher. As they were going out, they nearly collided with a tall, thin man in a dark suit and fez who came bustling in through the door. He bent over the stretcher.

'Do you want me to go with it?' he asked Mukhtar.

'Please, Mr Demeyrel. It's best if you get on with it as quickly as you can. The heat,' he explained to Seymour.

The three men left together.

Seymour looked round the room. It was small and dark and dirty and there were various bits of clothing scattered around. A dressing room, Seymour supposed.

'It is not nice here,' said Mukhtar, wrinkling his nose. 'Let us go somewhere else.'

As they were leaving the theatre, a small, harassed-looking man interrupted them.

'Can I use it?' he asked. 'The room, I mean?'

The terjiman nodded.

'I've finished here for the time being,' he said.

'This is terrible!' said the little man.

Mukhtar didn't say anything.

The little man seemed compelled to offer an explanation for wanting to use the room.

51

'It's the performance this evening. I mean, we've got to go on. And there are points when we need all the changing rooms.'

'If you're going on the way you have done,' said Mukhtar sternly, 'you're asking for trouble!'

The little man, who seemed to be the theatre manager, hung his head.

'There are only two of them,' he said. 'Now that Lalagé's gone.'

'Yes, well, they may not be so keen to continue now that they've seen what happened to Miss Kassim. However, that's not my business. I'm only interested in Miss Kassim.'

'I don't want you to think,' said the little manager, with sudden dignity, 'that I'm not.'

He stepped aside and they went on out. The crowd was still gathered at the foot of the steps.

'They're back,' Seymour heard someone say. 'The Fleshmakers.'

'They've never really gone,' someone else said.

The terjiman led Seymour down one of the dark alleyways. To his surprise they came out on the Galata Bridge. He hadn't realized it was so close. They went down some steps off to one side. Below the bridge was a large floating quay covered with stalls and booths. Some of the stalls, selling materials of various kinds, had spread their wares over the space between the shops. They seemed to cover every inch of the quay. From somewhere further along came the smell of frying fish.

Mukhtar stepped over the cloth and led him through a space between two of the stalls, so narrow that if you hadn't known it was there you would have missed it. At the end there was an area fenced off by four-feet high walls of carpet. Inside, there were low tables and at one end there were braziers on which a turbaned man was making coffee. They went to a table at the side. There were no chairs; they sat on the floor, and when Seymour did, he was conscious of the floor moving. The man at the end served them coffee in tiny cups, pouring from a tall copper pot with a long spout.

'I am sorry, Mr Seymour,' said Mukhtar, 'that you should, so soon after coming here, see the bad side of Istanbul.'

He spoke English well, although slightly over-correctly.

'It is what brought me here,' said Seymour.

Mukhtar nodded.

'Of course,' he said. 'And you will understand that it is not all like this.'

He sipped his coffee.

'And now to Miss Kassim. You were coming to see her, you said?'

'Yes. We had met yesterday evening. At the theatre. She came to our box at a point when she was not onstage.'

'And you arranged to meet her this evening?'

'After the performance, yes.'

'May I ask why? We are colleagues, Mr Seymour, and you can be frank.'

Seymour smiled.

'I was just hoping to talk to her,' he said. 'And I was not expecting, if that is what you are thinking, that it would lead to other things.'

'Forgive me. It was a possibility. May I ask what you were going to talk to her about?'

'Cunningham.'

'Ah, Cunningham.'

'She knew Cunningham, it appears.'

'Yes.' It did not seem to come as a surprise to him. 'And what, exactly, were you hoping that Miss Kassim could tell you about Cunningham?'

'I was hoping,' Seymour said, 'that she could give me a more rounded picture of him. All I have got so far is the Embassy side.'

The terjiman smiled.

53

'And she would, you hoped, be able to enlighten you about the other sides?'

'So I hoped.'

'They were, of course, lovers,' said Mukhtar.

'Were they?'

'There were others. She was one among many.' Was there a note of disapproval in his voice? 'But their relationship seems to have been particularly intense.'

'I did not know. For certain,' he added, not wishing to give too great an impression of ignorance. 'It was one of the things I wanted to find out.'

The terjiman nodded.

'And that was all?'

'All?'

'You did not wish to find out, for instance, how other sides of Miss Kassim's activities had been progressing?'

'Other sides?'

Mukhtar did not expand.

'No? Good. You were just, as you say, gathering information about Mr Cunningham's personal life. Well, if I can help, I would be glad to. We are, after all, colleagues, are we not?'

'We are, and I am most grateful to you for your offer of help. Please let me make it clear that I have no wish at all to intrude on your investigation. Nor to duplicate it. I am sure it will be conducted perfectly satisfactorily. It is just that, since Mr Cunningham was a British citizen, and, indeed, an official of His Majesty's service, certain enquiries have to be made.'

'Of course!'

'There are, too,' Seymour felt he could add, 'certain pressures at home in this case.'

Mukhtar smiled broadly.

'That, too, I can understand. And, as you can imagine, there are also pressures here.'

They both laughed. There was a kind of professional solidarity developing between them.

The terjiman glanced at his watch.

54

'I am afraid I must return to the theatre. There are other questions to be asked.'

'Of course!'

They went back along the tight little street, full now of the smells of people cooking their evening meal. From the smell it appeared that onions were going to figure largely.

'It is a pity,' said Mukhtar, 'about Miss Kassim. I was going to the theatre anyway today to see. There were some questions I wanted to put to her. Like yours,' he said, smiling, 'they were about Mr Cunningham. But now I shall not be able to put them.'

'Sadly, no.' Seymour thought for a moment. 'May I ask – does the fact that you were here to ask her some questions about him imply that you see a possible connection between the cases?'

'Possible? Well, possible, yes. But I have no firm view yet. The questions about Cunningham Effendi are one thing, and Miss Kassim's death, another. At the moment. All we know so far is that Miss Kassim is dead, apparently murdered.'

'May I ask how she was killed?'

'She was strangled. Probably, my colleague, Mr Demeyrel, suggests, with the string of a bow.'

'Bowstring?' said Seymour, startled, and with the words of the landau driver still fresh in his mind.

'Yes. Confirmation will have to wait until he performs his autopsy, because the string is so deeply embedded in the flesh that it is hard to tell with the naked eye. But, clearly, it is a very thin, hair-like cord of some kind, so thin that it is barely visible. Indeed, I myself did not see it until Mr Demeyrel pointed it out to me. He thought it might give an immediate lead to my enquiries.'

'Well, yes,' said Seymour, 'it would.'

'That is why I have to go back to the theatre. The band should be there now.'

'Band?'

'There will be string players among them.'

'Oh! *That* kind of bowstring!'

'Why, yes,' said Mukhtar puzzled. 'What kind did you think?'

That bloody landau driver, thought Seymour! With his bowstrings and Fleshmakers!

Squatting on the steps of the theatre was a small, dejected group of men.

'You are the band?' asked Mukhtar.

'To our misfortune, Effendi, we are,' said one, who appeared to be the leader.

'Which among you is the kemengeh player?'

'Oh, my God!' said one of the musicians despondently. 'Effendi, it is I.'

'Your name?'

'Farraj.'

'Have you your instrument with you?'

It was produced. Mukhtar examined it and then passed it politely to Seymour. It seemed to be a kind of viol, only short and thin, with a small bulb of a soundbox. On inspection, the bulb turned out to be a coconut, pierced with small holes and with about a quarter of it cut off. It stood, like a cello, on a long spike.

'And the bow,' said Mukhtar.

The bow seemed to Seymour pretty much like the ones used in England, only cruder. The horse-hair strings passed through a hole at one end and were tied to a ring at the other.

'I will take this,' said Mukhtar. 'Have you another?'

'Yes, Effendi,' said the depressed kemengeh player.

'With you?'

'Inside, Effendi.'

'Fetch it. Go with him,' Mukhtar said to one of the constables lounging nearby. 'Have you any spare strings? Bring them, too.'

They went off.

The band's leader plucked diffidently at the terjiman's sleeve.

'Effendi,' he said, 'the strings may not be that great. But this is not Farraj's fault. They are all he can afford. We are but poor men, Effendi, and we have to make do with what we can pay for.'

'The quality of the strings is not the issue,' said Mukhtar, looking round. 'Are there any more string players here? Does one of you play the 'ud?'

'Effendi –'

'Let me see it.' It appeared to be some kind of lute, played with a plectrum and not with a bow, but certainly a stringed instrument. 'I will keep that, too.'

'These bloody string players!' muttered one of the other musicians.

The string players gathered in a little group around the band leader. He turned to Mukhtar.

'Effendi,' he said, 'are you going to keep these instruments?'

'For a while, yes.'

'There is the performance tonight . . .'

Mukhtar considered.

'They will be returned to you before,' he said.

'Do better without them,' muttered the dissident.

'The kanum? Do you have a kanum?' demanded Mukhtar.

'Alas, Effendi . . . They hire by the band here. And the more players in the band, the less the money for each. We can get a kanum player if you wish, but you would have to pay extra.'

'That is not necessary. I wish to look only at the stringed instruments actually here. Are there any more? No?'

'I've always said you don't really need string players,' said the dissident.

'I will speak with you afterwards, Hassan,' hissed the 'ud player.

'Why don't you take his drums away, Effendi?' growled

57

the flute player. 'Then the music will be balanced and our ears will not be offended.'

'Ali –'

'I am interested only in the strings,' said Mukhtar hastily.

'There you are!' cried the drum player triumphantly. 'It is only the strings that are in question. The Effendi knows who plays the rubbish around here!'

'The quality of the strings is not the issue,' said Mukhtar firmly. 'Neither of the strings nor of the playing.'

There was a long silence.

'Then why –'

'The issue,' said Mukhtar 'is Miss Kassim.'

'Now, look, Effendi –'

'What goes on up on the stage is not our business –'

'Effendi, we are but simple players,' said the leader. 'Every night we come and make our music and then we go away again. What goes on up on the stage does not concern us. And if some of the turns are sinful –'

'Effendi, we ourselves were in doubt. They dress like men. They look like men. Who is to say they are not men?'

'Visit not their indecency upon us!'

'Shut up!' said Mukhtar. 'That is not the point. The point is, Miss Kassim has been murdered –'

'Murdered!'

'Have you not heard?'

'Miss Kassim? But, Effendi, we saw her only this afternoon. She was rehearsing –'

'That is right. And she went off to change. And while she was changing, she was murdered.'

They seemed stunned.

'And I am looking for the one that killed her,' said Mukhtar.

They struggled to take it in. And then:

'But, Effendi, why do you look among us?'

'Because it seems that she may have been killed by the string from a musical instrument.'

58

'I've always said that string players –' began the drum player swiftly.

'Shut up. Now, what I want to know is – and you would be wise to speak truly – did one of you go with Miss Kassim?'

'Effendi, we are upright men!'

'Effendi, we swear –'

'Never, Effendi!'

'None of you?' said Mukhtar sternly.

'None of us!'

'If only –' muttered someone at the back.

'Effendi,' said the band leader, 'she was too high for us. That is the truth of it. We are but poor men. She had other fish to fry.'

'Gold fish,' said someone.

'Gold fish?'

'She goes with rich men, Effendi, and does not spare a glance for such as we.'

Mukhtar looked around. The kemengeh player had not yet returned.

'What about Farraj? Did he not cast an eye on her?'

'Well, anyone can cast an eye –'

'But no more? Did he speak with her alone? Go to her room?'

'Farraj is an upright man –'

'And, anyway, he wouldn't have had a chance.'

'Effendi,' said their leader, 'whoever's string it was, it was not Farraj's.'

'That we shall see,' said Mukhtar.

'Lalagé?' said Rice-Cholmondely, the next morning, shocked. 'That's awful!'

He fetched Ponsonby.

'Yes, I know,' said Ponsonby. 'The notification has just come through.

'Already? That's quick off the mark. They must have someone intelligent on the case.'

59

'It's Mukhtar,' Seymour said. 'You know, the terjiman we met over at Gelibolu.'

'What's he doing over here? They usually stick to their own vilayet. Are you sure?'

'Quite sure. I had a long chat with him.'

'Someone will have to go down,' said Ponsonby.

'I will,' said Rice-Cholmondely.

'Mind if I come with you?' said Seymour.

'Why does someone have to go down?' asked Seymour, as they settled back in the landau.

'To collect her things.'

'And why should the Embassy be doing that?'

'She's a British passport holder.'

'With a name like Lalagé Kassim?'

'Well, the theatre business is a funny business. Out here, anyway.'

''Ello?' said an irritated, sleepy voice, in a strong East London accent.

'I'm from the Embassy,' said Rice-Cholmondely. 'I've come to collect Lalagé's things.'

The door opened and a tousled woman appeared, wearing a short nightdress.

'Got to bed late,' she said, apologetically. 'Come in.'

'Sorry about Lalagé,' said Rice-Cholmondely.

The woman shrugged.

'That's 'er bed,' she said, pointing. Underneath it was a battered suitcase. Rice-Cholmondely bent down and began to go through it.

'Why don't you just bloody take it?' said the woman.

'Got to check the individual things. They've all got to be signed for.'

'Oh, yes, everything's got to be bloody signed for!'

She sat down on the other bed.

'Have you roomed together long?' asked Seymour.

'Since we got 'ere. About eighteen months ago.'

'It must have been a shock,' he said sympathetically.

She didn't say anything. Her eyes, however, were red from crying.

'You got on well to share a room for that long.'

She shrugged.

'She was all right,' she said. 'You've got to stick together if you're a woman out 'ere.'

Rice-Cholmondely looked up.

'Anything else?' he said.

The woman stood up and took a worn dressing gown off a hook and threw it on to the bed.

'That's about it,' she said. 'We travel light.'

Rice-Cholmondely stuffed it into the case.

'Any family?' he asked. 'Anyone we could send this to?'

'Never 'eard of anyone.'

'We'll keep it in store. If you think of anyone, could you let us know?'

He handed her his card.

She looked at it, then put it away. There was a similar case below her bed.

'Does she owe anything? For the room, I mean?'

'We share it.'

'I'll look after it.'

He went out.

'Where are you from, then?' said Seymour.

'Bermondsey.'

'I'm Whitechapel.'

'Really?' she said, surprised. 'You don't sound it.'

'My family moved in,' he said.

She knew exactly what that meant.

'Immigrant, are you?'

'Way back. Grandfather's time.'

'What are you doing out 'ere, then? You're not one of them, are you?' She gestured in Rice-Cholmondely's direction.

'No. Police.'

'Police! Bloody 'ell!' Then, after a moment: 'You don't sound like one of them, either. 'Oo are you after?'

'A man named Cunningham. Know him?'

She nodded.

'I know 'im,' she said.

'He was killed, too.'

'Yes,' she said. 'I know. It seems to 'appen round 'ere, doesn't it?'

'Look, I'd like to talk to you. Alone. Can I take you out for coffee?'

She laughed.

'It's not like that,' she said. 'Not out 'ere. It's different for a woman, see.'

'Where can we go, then?'

'We can talk 'ere,' she said, 'after your mate's gone.'

Rice-Cholmondely came back up the stairs.

'That's all right,' he said. He picked up the suitcase.

'I'll stay here for a moment,' said Seymour. 'I'd like to have a word with this lady.'

'Nicole,' she said. 'That's my name. At least, it's my professional name.'

'Right. Nicole. Sorry about all this.' Rice-Cholmondely lingered for a moment. 'Nicole, there's probably no need to worry, but if I were you, I'd be a bit careful for a while. If you know what I mean.'

'I know what you mean,' said Nicole. 'I've been thinking that myself.'

'Right, then. See you later, old man. I shan't be going back just yet, so the landau will still be there for an hour or so.'

They heard his heavy feet on the stairs.

'You really Whitechapel? ' Nicole asked Seymour.

'Yes.'

'I quite like Whitechapel,' she said. 'There's more to it, isn't there, than there is to Istanbul. I mean, for a woman.'

*   *   *

She took off her nightdress and put on her working clothes, the clothes she rehearsed in. They were a man's clothes: baggy trousers and a loose shirt worn on top of the trousers and coming down to her knees. Under the shirt the shape of her breasts did not show. When she'd finished, and combed her hair, she sat down on the bed.

'They put 'er in the way of it, didn't they? I'm not saying they caused it, but if they 'adn't put 'er in the way of it, it wouldn't 'ave 'appened, would it?'

'They?'

'Those blokes up there. At the Embassy. Like 'im.' She gestured after the departed Rice-Cholmondely.

'How did they put her in the way of it?'

'There was this bloke. Really 'igh up, 'e was. A Prince or something. Well, that man Cunningham kept wanting 'er to be nice to 'im. You know what I mean? Well, she didn't mind. Not at first. I mean, 'e was rich, and 'e paid for what 'e got. And 'e was mad about 'er. Wanted to see 'er every night, you know, after the show. But, Christ, you've got to sleep sometime. And it was awkward. I mean, we shared the room. Of course, I didn't mind, we 'ad an arrangement, and I used to get out. But, Christ, every night! I mean, you want your own bed sometime, don't you. And there was always the rehearsal next morning.

'Well, it went on and on, and it got to the point when she didn't want to. Not every night. But 'e insisted, couldn't seem to let 'er go.

'"Look," I said, "you don't 'ave to if you don't want to. You can pull out." "Not so easy," she said. "And, besides, I quite fancy 'im." "Which one?" I said, because she'd always seemed keen on Cunningham. "Both!" she said, and laughed.

'"You silly cow," I said. "'E's using you." "I know," she said. "For Christ's sake," I said, "pull out of it." "I can't," she said, "not now." "You're crazy," I said. "Well, I am a bit," she said.

'You see, she was gone on that man Cunningham. 'Ad been from the first. I mean, 'e was a real charmer. Made 'er think she'd dropped out of 'eaven, just to please 'im. Well, she liked that. It was a bit of a change from the usual men she met. And, to be fair, 'e seemed quite keen on 'er.

'But then one evening 'e brought that Prince along, and 'e took a shine to 'er, too. Now you would 'ave thought 'e'd 'ave told 'im to clear off, although maybe you can't do that to a Prince. But 'e needn't 'ave gone as far as 'e did. 'E seemed positively to encourage it. 'E just laughed and said: "'Ere's your chance, Lalagé! Make a few bob out of 'im. Oh, and by the way . . ."

'I don't know what 'e wanted 'er to do by the way. Chat 'im up, certainly. But I think there was more to it than that. But I don't know what. She never said. Besides, I don't think she minded. In fact, she quite liked it, 'aving the two of them on a string, I mean. It made 'er fancy she was someone. Two men like that! One a Prince, the other, well, I don't know, but I'll tell you what, you don't see blokes like 'im in the East End! So she enjoyed 'erself and went round with 'er 'ead in the clouds.

'But I could see the others didn't like it. They didn't mind Cunningham, because 'e'd brought business in to the theatre. We'd shifted to a new level since 'e'd taken an interest in the theatre. Rudi was quite crazy about 'im – 'e'd eat out of 'is 'and. But the others, the ordinary people, the Turks, the porters and so on. They didn't like it.'

'What exactly was it that they didn't like?' asked Seymour.

''Er going around. Not so much with Cunningham, that didn't matter, but with the Prince. And doing it so openly! They thought she was flaunting it. You know, thrusting it in their face. I could see trouble coming and I said, "Lal, you want to watch it!" "I've got a powerful friend," she said. "'E'll take care of it." "You're earning yourself some powerful enemies," I said, "and they'll take care of *you*."'

Seymour asked her who the powerful enemies might be but she turned vague. She just felt it, she said. She *knew*. You ought to steer clear of these high-up blokes. Go too near the sun and you get burnt. Keep to your own level. Keep your head down. Don't stick your neck out. That was what she had learned, in Bermondsey as in the theatre. And out here, she said, it was even worse. Women didn't count for much out here. They were disposable. 'I mean, to the Sultan and them 'igh-ups. You get out of line and they send the Fleshmakers round.'

'The Fleshmakers?' said Seymour. 'I thought they were all in the past.'

'That's what Cunningham said. "They're all dead and gone, love," 'e said. "You can forget about them." But she shouldn't 'ave forgotten about them, should she?'

'I think there's something you should have told me,' said Seymour, as they were going back up the hill in the landau.

'Oh, yes, old chap?' said Rice-Cholmondely.

'About Lalagé. And Cunningham. What was she doing for him?'

'Don't quite know what you mean, old chap.'

'She was spying for him, wasn't she?'

Rice-Cholmondely was silent for a moment. Then:

'I wouldn't put it quite like that, old boy.'

'No? How would you put it, then?'

'More, gossip-collecting. Spying's not part of our job. Not as diplomats. But gossip-collecting is. Gossip can be very useful to us. It gives you a feeling for what's in the air, how you weigh things, read policy. A lot of a diplomat's work, you could say, is picking up gossip.'

'And that's what Lalagé was doing for you? Picking up gossip?'

'Yes. And the gossip that Lalagé picked up was particularly useful because it was Palace gossip.'

'Palace gossip?'

'The Palace positively buzzes with gossip, old boy. And it's important for us to have an in on it because that's where policy is made. And Lalagé had good contacts.'

'With a Prince?'

'Well, old boy, we won't go into it too much. Let's just say someone pretty high up. High enough to be really useful.'

'And that's all that Lalagé was doing? Picking up gossip?'

'That's all, old boy.'

'Cunningham was twisting her arm.'

'Cunningham was always a bit ruthless with women,' said Rice-Cholmondely, a little uneasily.

Chapter Five

A cavass brought him the letter while he was sitting outside on the terrace. Seymour had not been expecting a letter and was surprised. He was even more surprised when he looked at the letter. It had a little crest on the back and smelled of perfume. Seymour did not get letters like this.

He opened it. It contained two scented pages in a lady's neat, educated hand. He glanced at the signature: Sybil Cunningham.

Lady C.!

Dear Mr Seymour,

I was so pleased to hear that you are already in Istanbul. At last someone is moving. You won't believe how difficult it has been to get things started. In the end I had to go direct to Nicholas. He tried to fob me off with Lancelot. 'Don't try to hide behind your Foreign Secretary,' I said. 'You're the man in charge and I want to see something happen.' Of course, I did go and see Lancelot as well. In my experience of the British Government (which is extensive and a trifle unusual) it is important to *Follow Up*.

'Lancelot,' I said, 'don't you control your Ambassadors?' He huffed and puffed, of course. 'It's not a question of control,' he said. 'You mean they're out of control?' I said. 'I can well believe it, letting their staff get killed and doing nothing about it.' 'Something *is* being done about it,' he said. 'What?' I said. Well, he wriggled and said something about a report. 'Listen,' I said, 'if someone is murdered in England, you don't write reports, you send for the police.' 'It's not quite like that out there,' he said. 'I *want* it like that,' I said. Well, in the end he agreed to speak to Philibert. Naturally I spoke to Philibert first.

'You're in charge of the police, aren't you?' I said. 'Now send someone out there.' 'It's not as easy as that,' he said. 'I'll be in here tomorrow,' I said, 'and the next day and the next day until I find someone has gone.'

Well, of course, you can never rely on people at the top, so I spoke to a young nephew of mine at the Foreign Office, and he mentioned your name. Apparently he had come across you over something to do with Trieste. 'Send him,' I said. 'I have already,' he said. 'It's just a question of getting a few people above me to sign their names.'

Now Rupert is quite bright and I trust him. Which means that I trust you, Mr Seymour. However, just to make sure, I am thinking of coming out myself. I look forward to hearing about the progress you've made.

Yours sincerely,
Sybil Cunningham

P.S. I have a niece in Istanbul and I have written to her and told her to give you all the help she can.

S.C.

'Do I recognize that crest?' said Ponsonby, sitting beside him.

'It's from a Lady Cunningham.'

'Oh, yes. Cunningham's aunt.'

'She says she's coming out here.'

'My God!' said Ponsonby, going pale.

He jumped up and hurried across to the Ambassador.

'My God!' said the Ambassador. 'Sybil!'

Over on the far side of the terrace Felicity Singleton-Mainwaring was clutching at a piece of paper.

'Oh, crumbs!' she said. 'Aunt Syb!'

The Ambassador came over to Seymour.

'Seymour,' he said, 'how are you getting on? With this Cunningham thing, I mean.'

'Well, of course, I've only just started –'

'You don't think you could, well, speed it up, could you?'

Seymour went over to Felicity.

'Miss Singleton-Mainwaring –'

Felicity flinched.

'Don't call me that,' she said. 'It sounds so awful.'

'What shall I call you?'

'Felicity will do. That's pretty awful, too, but –'

'I wonder if you could help me?'

The next morning, early, she took him down to the Yacht Club and began to get her boat ready. Seymour stood and watched her. Sailing a boat was not among the skills of the Whitechapel police.

But it evidently was among Felicity's. The boat lay in a little slipway and in a moment she had pulled it down towards the open water, untied the straps and the rolled-up sail, and hoisted a little sail on the front. Then she held the boat while Seymour clambered in, cast off and let the little sail in front carry the boat out. Then she wedged the tiller between her knees and hoisted the mainsail. In another moment they were heading briskly out into the main channel and then were turning west towards the Dardanelles.

And then she undressed. Well, not completely.

'Can't manage in all this rig-out,' she said.

She took off her jacket and then her skirt. Beneath the jacket she was wearing a short-sleeved singlet. Under the skirt she was wearing pantaloon-like trousers.

'Much better for sailing in,' she explained. 'Although, of course, I have to make myself decent, by their standards, before coming in.'

The trousers came down to her calves and at some point she had slipped off her shoes, so that she was barefoot. It made her look more Eastern. In England, reflected Seymour, at least, in Victorian England, women showed their faces and were all coy about their ankles. In Turkey it was the other way round.

They were leaving Istanbul behind them. First to go were the boats, the caiques, dhows and feluccas. Next were the white houses scattered along the waterfront. Last of all were the domes and minarets which rose up above the city and gave it a cast very different from any city that Seymour was familiar with. The domes and minarets lingered for a long time but there was a moment at which he could see them all, both the foreign-looking boats and the unusual houses and the domes, and it was then that the Easternness of Istanbul came home to him.

The sun, once they were out on the sea, was brilliant. Literally; it flashed blindingly off the water and he began to regret that he had not purchased one of the ridiculous green eye-shades that he had seen people in the hotel wearing. The waves broke up in sparkles and the heat shimmered off the cliffs and above the barren, desert-like brown on the other side of the Straits. Earlier it had been fresh and green with little white houses poking out of it but that had given way to an unremitting brown.

He took off his jacket and tie and watched Felicity do the work.

'You're pretty good,' he said.

'It was either this or horses,' said Felicity.

'Horses?'

'For my family it was always horses. But I didn't like horses, and I didn't, actually, like my family much, so when we moved to Cornwall, I took up sailing. The good thing about sailing is that you can do it on your own and don't always have to have your family breathing down your neck.'

'Was that why you came out here? To Istanbul?'

'That and Gervase.'

70

'Gervase?'

'My family wanted me to marry him.'

'And you didn't?'

'I fled.'

'Why here?'

'Peter – he's my cousin, you know – was already out here. At the Embassy. And he said, "Why don't you come out here? No one in the family will have heard of Istanbul so they won't know where to find you. And none of our set will be out here, which will be a relief." But what clinched it was that there was good sailing. I was a little keen on Peter, too, of course, but that didn't last long, not when I actually got out here. A little of Peter goes a long way.'

Seymour wondered what she did for money. But maybe that was a daft thing to ask of the English rich.

'And now your family *is* coming after you,' he said.

'Aunt Syb!' said Felicity, shuddering. 'Although she doesn't really count as family. Not to the family, anyway. I mean, she sort of married in. Why, I can't imagine. I, personally, would prefer to marry out. As far out as I could get.'

'And Peter?'

'Exactly the same. That's why he chose the Diplomatic Service. "I want to get as far from England as I bloody can," he said. You see, he was always the brightest of us. Actually, he was the *only* one of us who had any brains. People wondered what he was doing among the Singleton-Mainwarings. That may be why Aunt Syb took to him. In fact, he was about the only one of us that she took to, except, for a time, Uncle Rog.'

'Uncle Rog?'

'Peter's father.'

'Now just let me get it clear about all these relationships –'

'Uncle Rog is Uncle George's brother, and Uncle George was married to Aunt Syb.'

'And where do you fit in?'

'There was a third brother. My Dad.'

'And Peter Cunningham was your cousin. And, presumably, there is at least one more cousin, since Aunt Syb had a child –'

'Richard. But she found him very disappointing. He was too much of a Singleton-Mainwaring. Took after his father.'

Seymour, lolling back against the side of the boat, admiring Felicity's expertise and also the trim figure taut against the singlet, found this illuminating. He thought he could see why Lady C. was so interested in Cunningham. But it was also illuminating about the Singleton-Mainwarings. How did a family like that get to be so near the top of the tree? Governor of the Bank of England, and so forth? Whereas Seymour's own family, and others in the East End like his, were so undeniably near the bottom of the tree?

Dullness, he thought, might be the answer. Their very dullness. Dullness was safe, reassuring. It did not rock any boats. But where, in that case, did Cunningham fit in? And Lady C.? Who seemed prepared to tip over every boat in sight.

It was a long journey down to Gelibolu, longer than he had thought. Felicity seemed quite happy about it, though, managing sails and rudder, in fact, doing all the work, which made Seymour quite happy, too. When he had seen her before, hearing her talk to the diplomats on the terrace, he had put her down as one of those gushy girls straight from a posh school, totally brainless but with the world at her feet, not at all Seymour's type. Seeing her now, though, so aware and so competent, and quite attractive, actually, now that she was, so to speak, stripped down, he began to revise his opinion.

'Shearwater?' he said, pointing to some birds on the top of the cliffs.

'Storks,' said Felicity.

Well, maybe Cunningham knew more about it than he did. However, they were about the only thing of interest on the cliffs. Fortifications? Gun emplacements? It all seemed pretty unlikely, even if it was in the future, as that military attaché had said. He was beginning to share Cunningham's opinion of Chalmers.

'Can you take us over to the other side?' he said. 'If you could find the exact place at which Cunningham put you down, that would be very helpful.'

The other side was about as bleak as the Abydos side, although less cliffy. Felicity took them in expertly and made the boat fast alongside a big, flat rock. Seymour stepped ashore.

'So,' he said, 'you were left here while Cunningham went off in the boat –'

'My boat,' said Felicity, still aggrieved. 'I was worried stiff. Not about him, but about the boat.'

They were on a sort of rocky point. The rock was so hot that it burned Seymour's feet through the soles of his shoes.

'It's baking, here,' he said, wiping the sweat from his face. 'What did you do while you were waiting for him?'

'Well, I tried to find some shade. I went up there,' said Felicity, pointing to a low overhang.

'Let's go up there.'

Close to, there were apparent paths.

'Goat tracks,' said Felicity. 'There were some goats here. And a man. He was supposed to be herding them but he was fast asleep when I came upon him.'

'And then what happened?'

'He gave a shriek and ran away. I think he thought,' said Felicity, embarrassed, 'that I was a houri.'

'Houri?'

'One of the girls of paradise. You know, when a Muslim dies and goes to paradise, that is, if he is a true believer, he is given a tent of pearls, jacinths and emeralds, and also seventy-two wives chosen from among the girls of paradise. Well, you know, dressed like this – I had taken off my skirt, you see, and my jacket, that's how I always sail –

73

I think he thought – and, being a bit different, you know, pale-skinned and foreign – Anyway, he shouted, "Oh, my God, a houri!" and bolted up the cliff.'

There were some goats around now.

They climbed up one of the tracks to the top and found an old man lying on the ground. His eyes widened when he saw them, especially when he saw Felicity.

'Again!' he cried. 'Oh, my God!'

He would have run away if Seymour had not been there.

'Ana mush houri!' said Felicity hastily, which Seymour worked out to be, I am not a houri. The old man seemed faintly reassured. Felicity went on talking.

'You speak Arabic?' said Seymour.

'A bit,' said Felicity, blushing. 'Peter says it's white man's Arabic, boss Arabic. But I can't help that, can I? And it gets by.'

'That's terrific!' said Seymour. 'Now, look, can you ask him some things for me?'

Through Felicity he was able to establish that the goat-herd came regularly to this spot. He had, of course, seen Felicity when she had come here before and had, indeed, watched her from afar the whole time she had been on the rock. He remembered Cunningham returning and picking her up.

'Does he remember Cunningham coming again?'

Yes, the old man did. At least, he said he did. But what he reported seemed, well, unlikely at the very least. Cunningham had come, he said, not in one boat but in two. One was a small rowing boat, tied on behind the back of a larger felucca. Two men had got out of the felucca, got into the small boat and started rowing.

'Are you sure?' said Seymour. 'Is he right about this? Wasn't one of the men swimming?'

Well, he was. The old man hadn't liked to say so because he had thought they wouldn't believe him. But, lo and behold, and God is great (Seymour got that bit), one of the men had slipped over the side of the boat into the sea

74

and begun to swim. 'Like a dolphin.' The goatherd had thought he might be a god, or at least a djinn. The strangest things were happening on this part of the coast. Out he had swum, like a dolphin, and the small boat had gone with him. He had watched them until they had disappeared; he assumed, into paradise, especially when he had seen, shortly after, a large cargo ship going past.

What about the felucca? The felucca had stayed where it was, moored close in, until it had started to get dark, when it had put out again. Once the man had got back.

Once the man had got back? The swimmer?

No, no, the man who had got out of the felucca. After the other boat had left. He had got out of the felucca and walked to the town. Sestos. Where he had had a haircut.

This was the bit where the account had started to seem unlikely. Not to say bizarre. But the goatherd was adamant. The man had got out of the felucca and walked off in the direction of Sestos. And he knew about the haircut because he came from Sestos himself and when he had gone there the next day to take a young goat to Mustafa's, he had talked with Mustafa about the man, and Mustafa had told him he had gone to have a haircut, and the goatherd had doubted this – why would a fine man go to a man such as Ibrahim for a haircut? – and Mustafa had told him to go and talk to Ibrahim, and he had, and Ibrahim had confirmed it. (And added, why should not a rich man come to him, Ibrahim? Was he not known far and wide as a true barber? And the goatherd had agreed that he was, but had still marvelled.)

Okay, so he had gone to Sestos to have a haircut, let's say, for the time being, thought Seymour: what then? Then he had come back to the felucca and climbed aboard and the felucca had sailed off.

'Was that all?' said Seymour.

'All?'

'What about the woman?'

'Woman?'

75

Hadn't there been a woman? Left on the rock? Or perhaps she had stayed on board the felucca?

'A woman,' said Felicity encouragingly.

'At my age,' he said, 'one houri is enough!'

Haircut? It seemed unlikely. But there was one way of checking.

'How far is it to Sestos?' he said.

The barber's shop was a chair in the street. Beside it were some bowls and, standing in the dust, a row of shaving brushes. Laid out beside them on a not altogether clean piece of towelling was an array of razors of the cut-throat variety. On another piece of towelling were some combs, shaving soap and several pairs of scissors.

The chair was empty at the moment and the barber himself was squatting in the dust chatting to a circle of cronies.

Seymour went up to him and gestured questioningly towards the chair.

'Ibrahim,' said one of the cronies, 'your day is made!'

The barber leaped up. He seized a cloth and dusted the chair.

'Effendi,' he said, 'you have come to the right place.'

'I hope so.'

'A shave? A refreshing shave? Just the thing on a hot day!'

'A trim, please. Just a trim. What's the Arabic for trim?' he asked Felicity.

'Lord!' said Felicity. 'I don't know.'

'Trim?' said the barber. 'I know just what you need, Effendi. There . . . and here . . .'

'Not too much!' warned Seymour.

'Effendi, you will not know the scissors have touched. But, afterwards, your head will be radiant!'

'Yes, well, thank you. Just a trim, please.'

The scissors began to snip. The group of onlookers, larger now, watched admiringly. 'Make it good, Ibrahim,' advised a man sitting at the front of the circle. 'This is no ordinary man who is before you. It is not every day that you cut the hair of a foreign Effendi.'

'Oh, I don't know,' said Ibrahim airily.

'The rich men beat a path to your chair,' said another man, enviously.

'Well, yes, that is true.'

'You have had other rich men?' asked Seymour, including himself, for the first time, in the category.

'Only the other day, Effendi, a man came to me, dressed like a Prince, and sat down in the chair, just like that, and said, "Short back and sides!"'

'Ibrahim –'

'It is true,' insisted the barber. 'As true as that I stand here. I wondered at first if he might be a djinn, for he came out of the desert. But then he said, "Get on with it, or you'll feel the toe of my shoe up your backside," so I knew he was a Prince.'

'Did he pay like a Prince?' asked someone sceptically.

'I'm not complaining,' said the barber offhandedly.

'He must have been crazy,' declared the sceptic. 'Coming here when he could have gone to one of the big shops in Istanbul!'

'I expect he liked the personal touch,' said the barber.

'Or maybe he couldn't find anyone else at the time. You know how it is with these rich people. It's always got to be "Now!" with people like that. I expect he was just passing by when the idea struck him. "Have a haircut!" And he looked around and saw Ibrahim. Lucky Ibrahim!'

'What would a man like that be doing "just passing"? A place like Sestos? In the middle of the desert?'

'He came in a felucca,' someone else said. 'Old Ali, the goatherd, told me. And then he walked over here.'

'Walked over here? A man like that? You'd have thought he'd at least have had himself carried.'

'Well, you never know with rich men. They get these ideas –'

'He really was a Prince, though,' someone put in. 'The felucca had a green flag and gold tassels. Old Ali told me.'

'It must be Prince Selim, then,' someone said. 'He's the only one with a felucca.'

'A Prince! Here!'

'In my chair,' said the barber, modestly.

'You would have thought,' grumbled Felicity, as they walked back to her boat, 'that after making all that fuss about having a Hero to swim to, he would at least have had one! I mean, I would have done it if he'd asked. It would have been better than nothing. But perhaps he thought that cousins wouldn't count?'

'You would have counted for me,' said Seymour.

'Would I?' said Felicity, pleased, and going slightly pink.

They found Felicity's boat bobbing peacefully at anchor beside the rocks. The old goatherd was nowhere to be seen, but in the distance there was the faint bleating of goats.

The wind was behind them on the way back, which was just as well, because it was dark by the time they reached the Yacht Club.

Seymour took Felicity out to dinner as a reward; which was more, she pointed out, than Cunningham had ever done.

They chose a rather posh, Western-style restaurant, where, said Felicity, women were less likely to be viewed askance. There were, in fact, few women at the tables but enough to make Felicity feel comfortable.

It was only when they were some way on in their meal

78

that Seymour noticed Mukhtar, sitting in an alcove with three other men. Mukhtar caught his eye at the same moment and immediately jumped up and came across to them.

Seymour introduced Felicity as Cunningham's cousin.

Mukhtar gave a flicker of surprise but then bowed, in a nice, old-fashioned way, over Felicity's hand and said how sorry he was about her cousin. He went back to his table but returned a little later and invited them to join him and his friends for coffee.

The friends, all young, slim and trim, as Mukhtar was, rose and welcomed them with smiles; although Seymour noticed that they seemed a bit awkward with Felicity, addressing their remarks to Seymour and shyly avoiding looking Felicity in the face. (Felicity told him afterwards that it was probably because they had never seen a woman without a veil before.)

They were in general, though, very Westernized, talking with enthusiasm about things Western, which they equated with things modern. The Ottoman Empire, they said, needed to change. It was too locked in the past. As the discussion continued, they lost their self-consciousness and became more and more excited. (Felicity said afterwards that this was the way it often was in young Ottoman circles, that ideas excited them.) Seymour thought it was refreshingly different from England, where ideas seemed to excite no one. Although perhaps it was different in university towns.

He had assumed that they were university students but they said no, it was hard to sustain a university course if you didn't have money. No, they said, they were at one of the army schools for young officers, which meant, they said, smiling, that they got paid while they were studying.

Mukhtar seemed a little older than they were, and Seymour asked if he had gone to an army school, too, before taking up his job.

Mukhtar said yes, but didn't seem inclined to expand:

but then he said, yes, but he had been to law school as well and also studied languages. Seymour was impressed by this. The post of terjiman was obviously a more considerable one than he had taken it for; and he was a little surprised to find Mukhtar involving himself with something so lowly as the investigation of the murder of an actress in some little theatre.

As Seymour was walking Felicity back to her apartment he asked her where she had learned her Arabic and Turkish.

'Nowhere, really,' said Felicity. 'I just sort of picked them up.'

'You must have a facility for languages.'

'Gosh, no!' said Felicity, overwhelmed by the thought. But then, a little later, she said that perhaps she had.

'The trouble is, though,' she said, 'it doesn't help.'

'With what?'

'With what I am going to do with my life. I mean, I can't do a job or anything. Because I'm a woman. If I was a man I could go into the Foreign Office. Like Peter did. He was good at languages, too. But they don't take women. Nor do the banks, nor any of the businesses here. Neither here nor, as a matter of fact, in England. I would like to be an interpreter, a proper one, I mean. But you,' said Felicity, blushing, 'you are the only person I've had a chance to interpret for.'

'I was an interpreter once,' said Seymour. 'In the East End. Before I became a policeman.'

'Gosh!' said Felicity, wide-eyed. 'How marvellous!'

Seymour had liked his work as an interpreter; but he had never thought of it as marvellous. With Felicity leaning towards him, however, he was rapidly persuaded and told her about the kind of things he had done.

'Golly!' said Felicity. 'How terrific!'

'It wasn't as terrific as all that,' said Seymour hastily. 'It was terribly badly paid.'

'I wouldn't mind that.'

'Well, no. But my father did. He was having to support me. After a year or two he said, "Were you thinking of earning a living sometime?" And it was just at that time that the offer came from the police. I'd done a lot of work for them, you see, and suddenly they noticed me. "You're a bright lad," they said. "Why don't you join us?" I jumped at the chance. It was a big step up from being an interpreter. That,' said Seymour, 'is how low an interpreter was.'

But Felicity didn't seem to take the point.

'An interpreter!' she said dreamily. 'In the East End! How fabulous!'

Chapter Six

The next morning he went to the Embassy and found Rice-Cholmondely and together they made a list. Then they worked through it.

'Elsie Faversham?'

'I don't think so, old boy. Standing on a rock? Wouldn't that attract attention? They wouldn't have wanted that. What with her husband –'

'Ulla Svensson?'

'Doubtful, old boy. I mean, she's Diplomatic. At least, her husband is. Would stir up no end of trouble. Got to be discreet, old boy, if you're in the Diplomatic. And standing on a rock beside the Dardanelles . . .'

Seymour sighed. They had already been through fifteen names on the list of Cunningham's lovers, and to each of them Rice-Cholmondely had raised objections.

'Fatima?'

'No, no. She's the wife of . . . well, a very senior man at the Sultan's court. You just don't do things like that if you're an Ottoman wife. Stand on a rock for all to see? Look, being out anywhere with a man is bad enough. You'd be dead in five seconds and so would he.

'The fact is, old boy, women don't do that sort of thing. Not out here. You've got to behave yourself in public. That is, if you're a woman. And making an exhibition of yourself beside the Dardanelles . . .' Rice-Cholmondely shook his head. 'No respectable woman –'

'Ah,' said Seymour, 'but suppose she wasn't respectable?'

'Cunningham was a member of the British Embassy,' said Rice-Cholmondely stiffly.

'How about the actresses in the theatre?' said Cunningham. 'He went in for them, didn't he? They're not respectable. And they might have been glad of the part.'

'Wouldn't it have been difficult for them to get away?' objected Rice-Cholmondely. 'At that time? Wouldn't they have been due onstage?'

'It might have been possible for one of them to get away. Lalagé, for instance.'

Rice-Cholmondely was unconvinced.

'Can't see it, old boy. Too big a hole in the cast.' He was silent for a moment or two. Then he said, 'There's Leila, of course.'

'Leila?'

But then Rice-Cholmondely shook his head.

'Can't see it, though. Can't see her waiting for anybody. And certainly not on a rock beside the Dardanelles. Not her sort of place, old boy. Now, the Grande Rue, perhaps –'

'At least she seems a possible. Where could I find her?'

'In the Fields of the Dead, old boy. About four o'clock. Any afternoon.'

As they went out on to the terrace for coffee Seymour heard faint sounds of music from somewhere deep in the recess of the Embassy. The uncertain chords suggested a quartet.

'The Embassy Chamber Music Ensemble,' said Rice-Cholmondely. 'The Old Man's very keen on it. He plays second violin.'

Some time later the quartet emerged to join the others on the terrace. There was the Ambassador, pleased; the first violin (actually, quite a good player), grim; the viola, depressed; and Felicity, flustered, with cello.

'I don't really play,' she confided to Seymour, 'but

83

they're short of a cello and I did play at school. Only in the junior orchestra, though.'

'You play very determinedly, Felicity,' said the Ambassador, encouragingly. 'Everyone had their coffee? How about another go?'

'Not this morning, I'm afraid,' said the first violin. 'I've got a meeting.'

'What a pity!' said the viola, emerging suddenly from his depression.

'A pity!' echoed Felicity, with relief.

'Oh, well . . . Tomorrow, then? Afternoon?'

'I didn't realize that the Embassy was so keen on music,' said Seymour.

'It is,' said Ponsonby darkly, 'and that's why it's less than keen on the Ensemble.'

'And where,' asked Seymour, his mind still on Cunningham, 'did Cunningham stand on this?'

'As far away as possible,' said Ponsonby, picking up his cup and a file of papers he was working on, and going inside.

'Felicity,' called the Ambassador, 'the landau's ready when you are.'

'Oh, thanks,' said Felicity, picking up her cello. 'It's such a business walking when you're carrying a cello,' she said to Seymour.

'Do you mind if I come with you?' said Seymour.

'My brother is also a musician,' announced Ibrahim, the coachman, as he stowed the cello away and helped Felicity up into the landau.

'Oh, yes? And what does he play?' asked Felicity.

'The kaval.'

He put his hands to his mouth and made as if to blow.

'He's a worried man, though, is my brother,' said Ibrahim, getting up into the driver's seat.

84

'Oh? Why?'

'He plays in the theatre band, you see, and there was a woman murdered there the other night, strangled, the police say, with a string from a musical instrument. Of course, everyone knows that she was strangled with a bowstring and that it was the Fleshmakers who did it. But the police want to cover that up, so it's the band that's going to get it in the neck. No, no, not the neck, exactly, at least, not like her, that is. But they all think that the band will be blamed.'

'Yes, but your brother should be all right,' said Seymour. 'If he plays the –'

'Yes, but the police don't know the difference between a kemengeh and a kaval. They're all the same to them, just musical instruments. And, anyway, what does it matter, so long as *someone* is caught and blamed? That's what my brother says, and he's afraid it might be him.

'I tell him that he might be better off in prison. I mean, if the Fleshmakers are on the prowl. Although, of course, they might be just after women. You know, one of *those* women, indecent ones. In which case he would be all right.

'But he says they might not just be after a woman, which no one would mind, but after the theatre in general. You know, for having women on the stage, and all the other sins that go on. There's plenty of that, I can tell you. And that's what I said to my brother. "That's the sort of place the theatre is," I said, "and always will be. You'd best be out of it." "I need a job," he says. "Well, you find some other one," I say. "Because if the Fleshmakers have got wise to what's going on there, they'll be back, you mark my words. And it won't be long before the band is running out of strings."'

'My cousin tried to play the saz,' said Felicity, as she settled back in the landau. 'Peter,' she said to Seymour.

'Saz very difficult,' said Ibrahim.

'I know. Peter used to go for lessons to an old saz player in the band.'

'Saz player in band?' said Ibrahim.

'I know it's unusual. He wasn't in the band at first. He used to play to the people outside waiting to come in. But Peter heard him and told the theatre they ought to employ him. "He's the genuine article," he said. "He's special." Well, they used to listen to Peter at the theatre so they did what he said. The trouble was, they didn't know much about music and they put him with the band. The band nearly walked out.'

'Why was that?'

'Well, it's a very different sort of music. People who play the saz are folk musicians. They sing and play on their own. I don't think Peter ever thought he should play *in* the band. But he thought he was so good that they ought to make use of him somehow, perhaps as an individual turn.

'But they just shoved him in with everyone else. The band didn't like it and was forever causing trouble and in the end the theatre got rid of him. But while he was there, Peter used to go to him for lessons.'

'Not possible learn saz,' said Ibrahim. 'Not for Englishman. Need soul.' He beat on his chest. 'Turkish soul. Cunningham Effendi not Turkish. Impossible! The saz plays for the Turkish heart. Saz music comes from inside. Deep, deep inside. And from past. From Turkey as it was once, not as is now. Days when Sultan was well, Sultan. Foreigners play? No, not possible. Saz Turkish. Speak for Turkey.'

Seymour got out of the landau at the bottom of the hill and made his way through the narrow, dark, crowded streets to the theatre. Mukhtar was standing on the steps talking to someone. Seymour hung back for a moment not wishing to interrupt.

The person Mukhtar was talking to was a youth of about

seventeen, or so it seemed to Seymour, and the conversation didn't seem to be going smoothly. The terjiman was plainly irritated and the boy sulky. Seymour guessed that he must be a member of the theatre's troupe, for he seemed partly in greasepaint. At any rate, he was wearing dark eyeshadow.

Seymour couldn't hear what they were saying and probably wouldn't have been able to understand it anyway, since they were talking in Arabic. All he could go by was the dumb show and there was plenty of that. The boy was defiant and everything he did, from the languid, almost insolent way he stood to the bored expression on his face, seemed calculated to annoy. It was a good case of what the sergeant in the Whitechapel police station would have called dumb insolence.

And if he was trying to provoke the terjiman, he was certainly succeeding. Seymour could see Mukhtar's irritation even from where he was standing. Eventually he pushed the youth angrily aside and went up the steps into the theatre. Behind his back the youth saluted him mockingly.

Seymour asked one of the attendants if Nicole was rehearsing. Not at the moment, the man said; they were taking a break. He said he would look for her, and shortly afterwards she came out.

Seymour apologized.

'I don't want to interrupt whatever you're doing,' he said.

'You're not. I could do with some air, and I could do with a fag, too, but they don't like women smoking.'

They went round the corner of the theatre and Nicole squatted down in the shade, exactly like the old women sitting in the doorways cutting up vegetables.

'Don't tell me!' she said. 'It's my bright eyes you've come to see. You just couldn't stay away.'

'That's it!' said Seymour. 'How did you guess?'

They both laughed.

'So . . .' she said.

'A question I wanted to ask,' said Seymour.

'About Lalagé?'

'It might be. It starts with Cunningham, though.'

'That bastard!'

'You know his plan to swim the Straits?'

'Who doesn't?' said Nicole.

'Part of it was to have a woman he was swimming to.'

'A Hero, yes.'

'You know about that?'

'Yes, yes,' said Nicole wearily.

'Did he ask Lalagé to do it?'

'Play Hero, you mean?'

'Yes.'

'Well, 'e asked.'

'And she said no?'

'She was tempted. The way 'e put it. "Your chance!" 'e said. "To play a really big part! It's like Cleopatra. A leading role! You can be a star for once in your little life. The world will be looking at you, Lalagé. Or I bloody will by the time I've swum across!"

'"It's crazy!" I told 'er. "You don't want to 'ave anything to do with it. 'E'll probably drown, or one of those big boats will go over 'im, and then where will you be? Stuck on those bloody rocks!" In the end she said no, but it wasn't because of that. It was because 'e wanted 'er to do it in the evening, when she would 'ave been onstage. "You'll lose your job," I said. "And then where will you be? Who's going to pay the rent?"'

'So she didn't do it?'

'No.'

'Did he ask anyone else to do it? Anyone else in the cast?'

'There were only three of us. Three girls, I mean. The other one is Monique, but she couldn't do it. She can't stand the sun. It's 'er complexion, she's very fair. The sun is really bad for 'er, it makes 'er face come up in blotches. And then, of course, she can't go onstage.'

'What about you?'

'Did 'e ask me, you mean?' She laughed. 'Swim across to me? 'E wouldn't even spit in my direction. We didn't get on. I've met people like 'im before. So superior they wouldn't even give you the time of day! Unless they wanted something from you, and then they'd be all over you. I've been around too long to fall for that. You give them what they want and when they've 'ad it, they drop you in the ditch. So, no, 'e didn't ask me and I wouldn't 'ave done it if 'e 'ad.'

The youth was still lounging on the steps.

'You're in trouble, Nicole,' he said maliciously. 'They've started your piece.'

'Oh, Christ!' said Nicole, and hurried inside.

The youth laughed and then went after her. As he was going in, he nearly bumped into Mukhtar, who was coming out. He stepped aside and made him a mock bow. Then he shot off inside, leaving the terjiman in a fury again.

'These people!' he said to Seymour. 'I do not understand these people!'

'Theatre people, you mean?'

'Them, too,' said Mukhtar. 'But, no, I meant khawals.'

'Khawals?'

'Dancing boys. They dance at weddings and on occasions like that. At popular entertainments. There is a long tradition of such people. It is dying out now but the old people like them. But there are some who even when they are not dancing put kohl around their eyes and henna on their hands and keep their hair long like women, and those we call ginks. That boy,' said Mukhtar, 'is a gink!'

'I see. Yes.'

'It is not seemly,' said the terjiman, with unexpected

89

vehemence. 'It is not becoming. That boy! Has he no pride? No spirit of manliness?'

'Well . . .'

'Some of them even wear veils!' said Mukhtar bitterly.

'Yes. Well . . . But, of course . . .'

'I know. What does it matter? And, besides, it is traditional. There have always been dancing boys, people say, and why shouldn't there be? Their dancing gives pleasure. There are two principles in dancing, a friend of mine says, the masculine one and the feminine one, and in dance one plays against the other. Without them both a dance is incomplete. As in life. But without the dancing boy, how is the feminine to be expressed? You can't have women, of course, so . . .'

He shrugged.

'Well, I don't know,' he said. 'I don't know about these things. I am not an expert. To me it seems . . . Well, the practice is dying out, anyway. Let it die of its own accord, they say. Well, if that is what is happening, so be it.

'But ginks, that is a different matter. For they do not reserve their behaviour for private entertainments. They show themselves in public, and that is bad, for it affronts the old and is a bad model for the young. There should be no place for people like that in a modern Turkey. In the Turkey we are trying to build.'

Seymour was surprised. It was a different side of Mukhtar that he was seeing: different in more ways than one. He felt, however, compelled to register a mild objection.

'Well, yes, but perhaps in the theatre . . .?'

The terjiman shook his head.

'Not even in the theatre. And certainly not in this theatre at this time when it is so much in the public eye.'

'Is it in the public eye?'

'Oh, yes. And dangerously. It stands out in so many ways compared with other theatres.'

'Women on the stage?'

'Yes. For one thing. Our society is changing, becoming

more modern. But there are still many who do not like such things and see them as a deep affront to their religion. However, there are other things, too. You know – or perhaps you don't know – that this theatre has taken on a political tack. It has become satirical, it makes political attacks. Well, nothing wrong with that, you may say. You are, perhaps, used to that sort of thing in Europe. But out here people are not used to it. It makes them angry. And so, for a variety of reasons, the Theatre of Desires is under attack.'

'When you say, under attack –'

'There is much general hostility towards it, expressed mostly in threats and abuse. But I can't help wondering –'

He broke off.

'Well,' he said, 'it occurs to me that Miss Kassim would be especially vulnerable to the expression of that hostility.'

Rice-Cholmondely had agreed to take Seymour to the Fields of the Dead that afternoon and, punctually at four, they set off down the hill in the landau.

Les Petits Champs des Morts, the Fields of the Dead, were about halfway down Pera Hill. And fields of the dead they definitely were. It was a vast cemetery.

The brown, arid land stretched away on all sides, littered with white gravestones scattered all over the place and at all angles, white against brown; like almonds, thought Seymour, in a coffee-coloured mousse. White columns stood up occasionally like old teeth. Here and there cypresses bowed over the graves like the dark feathers he still sometimes saw on horses at East End funerals.

'They come here to eat sweets,' said Rice-Cholmondely.

'Sweets?'

'Of course, they shouldn't really eat in public at all. It's improper. But out here among the tombs, it's . . . well, condoned. So the Istanbul ladies seize the opportunity. Of

91

which, of course, there are few if you are an Istanbul lady.'

The tombs were often quite substantial, indeed, more like houses. They even had windows. Seymour peeped in one and got a surprise. The house was furnished. Carpets covered the walls, low divans stood on the marbled floor, brightly coloured glass lamps hung from the ceiling.

'They obviously wanted to make sure they were going to be comfortable.'

'Yes, indeed,' said Rice-Cholmondely. 'But, of course, this was intended not so much for them as for their families when they came to visit them. On certain festivals families foregather to remember the dead. They bring food and have a sort of picnic. It's all very jolly.'

And jolly, too, Seymour thought, were the cages over some of the smaller graves with songbirds fluttering in them to entertain the spirit of the departed.

Jolly, yes, but . . . what was Leila doing here? Apart from eating sweets?

'Really, of course, they're here to meet their lovers.'

'Here? In a cemetery?'

'Well, of course, there are not many places in Istanbul where you *can* go if you want to meet a man alone. You have to have an excuse to go even where men might be. And what better excuse than to go to pray for the dead? Very devout, Istanbul ladies are.'

And, indeed, as they penetrated further into the vast cemetery, there *did* seem to be a lot of women.

Most of them were dressed in the usual long, shapeless black gown of the ordinary Turkish woman, with dark veils to cover the face and a dark mantle to cover the hair – hair, Rice-Cholmondely assured him, was considered dangerously provocative to youth.

Some, however, were dressed in the height of Parisian fashion, which Seymour thought likely to be even more provocative to youth. They still wore black and covered their heads with mantles and their faces with veils but the veils were somehow skimpy, often nearly transparent, and,

Seymour thought, rather fetching. But how did they manage with the Turkish Delight?

Ahead of them as they walked through the graves was a particularly elegant group of pencil-thin ladies all dressed dutifully in dark and suitably veiled. But the lines of the dresses were definitely Parisian and the cut of the veil was hardly designed to conceal.

'There she is!' cried Rice-Cholmondely.

Others had their veil hanging properly down from the mantle, concealing the eyes; Leila's, somehow, was draped about the lower part of the face. A pair of dark, intelligent eyes looked over the top of it.

'What is this?' she said, looking at Seymour. 'A new one?'

'Seymour is just here temporarily,' said Rice-Cholmondely.

'But why just temporarily?'

'He has come here to look into something.'

'Oh, yes? And what, exactly?'

'And then he goes home again,' said Rice-Cholmondely firmly.

Leila laughed.

'A secret, is it? Let me guess.' The dark eyes studied Seymour curiously. 'Is it something to do with Cunningham?'

Not much was secret here, thought Seymour. At least to the Istanbul ladies.

'You knew Cunningham?' he asked.

'Only too well, said Leila grimly.

'I think,' said Seymour, after they had been walking for a while, 'that you might be worth swimming the Straits for.'

'Swimming . . .? Ah, that foolish story!'

'You weren't the one he swam it for?'

'I won't say I wasn't tempted when he asked me. It was such a splendidly romantic thing to do. And I, I am very romantic.'

'But nevertheless . . .?'

'I did not believe him.'

'You did not think he would actually do it?'

'Oh, I thought he would do it, all right. It's exactly the sort of thing that he would do.'

'Then . . .?'

'But I didn't think he would be doing it for the reason he said. Cunningham was not, actually, a very romantic man. Oh, he talked a lot about romantic things. But it was usually when he was wanting to get you to do something for him. Like get into bed with him. He was actually very calculating. You always felt that really he had something else in mind. You know, you felt that when he was making love to you, all he was really wanting to do was exercise his back! A woman doesn't like that. At least, not a romantic woman like me.'

She gave him a quick look.

'Perhaps you do not think I am romantic?'

'Oh, I'm sure you are.'

'Well, I am. And certainly when I make love I am romantic. Everything in me is involved. No part hangs back. I am all there. A woman is like that. She is total. But a man . . . or, at least, Cunningham . . .'

'And that was why you refused when he asked?'

'Well, not entirely. For I am realistic, too. And I did not want to stand for hours on a hot bit of rock, with crabs and scorpions coming at me.'

They walked on for a little while and then Rice-Cholmondely came to a halt.

'Leila, dear, enchanting as is your company, I think we ought to be getting back.'

'But what is the point of going through the Fields of the Dead,' enquired Leila, 'if you do not go on to the Valley of the Sweet Waters?'

94

Rice-Cholmondely glanced at his watch.

'It would take us another hour at least . . .'

Leila put her arm through Seymour's.

'I wish particularly to show Mr Seymour the Valley of the Sweet Waters,' she said.

The Valley of the Sweet Waters of Europe lay just beyond the cemetery. Until a century ago, Leila said, its slopes had been covered by pleasure domes and pavilions and gardens full of pomegranates and peaches and apricots. There had been rills crossed by rustic bridges and shady glades where hundreds of herons built their nests. In the giant plane trees the nightingales sang unceasingly.

Or so said Leila.

There were still trees and streams and paths with bridges but today the pleasure domes were in ruins and down at the edge of the sea the palaces of the pashas had been replaced by oil tanks, docks and wharves. But still, said Leila, the people came and walked in the shade: the Muslims on Fridays and the Christians on Sundays.

'And what they are seeing,' said Leila, 'is pleasure domes and pavilions.'

'And what they are doing,' said Rice-Cholmondely, 'is making assignations among the trees.'

'That,' said Leila, 'is a very Cunningham style of thinking.'

They came to a place where there were two bridges. Seymour and Leila went over one and Rice-Cholmondely, together with Leila's companions, over the other, thinking they would meet on the other side of the street. In fact, the paths diverged for a while. Seymour took advantage of the separation to talk without Rice-Cholmondely hearing.

'Why did you say that you knew Cunningham only too well?'

Leila was silent for a moment. Then she said, 'He involved me in something which at first I thought was full of wonderful possibilities for me. But then, actually, it turned out to be rather nasty.

'There was a Prince he was friendly with. They had met in Europe when Cunningham was serving at an Embassy there, in Berlin, I think, and became very friendly. And then when Cunningham came out here, and the Prince returned, they picked up the friendship again. At first it was a question of the Prince showing Cunningham round, but soon it was the other way. The Princes don't know much about Turkey, or even about Istanbul, they're very isolated, and Cunningham soon knew quite a lot. He had a gift for immersing himself in a country, was always very interested – genuinely interested, he wasn't just pretending – in its culture. So soon it was he who was showing the Prince round. He introduced him to things – mosques he had never seen, theatres. People, too.'

'Women?'

'Yes.'

'You?'

'Yes. At first I was very flattered. A Prince, after all. The highest I'd got before were pashas and Embassy people. This opened up a new world for me. Or so I thought. He seemed to like me. A lot. He was always coming round to my place. Almost every day. And he seemed very nice. He was courteous, you know, and considerate. Not like most men out here. And he was royal, too! I couldn't get over that. To be royal and yet to be so considerate.

'He'd been to school in England, you know, and perhaps to university there. He seemed very British; indeed, more British than the British. Rather like those men at the Embassy, correct, polite, always very polite, indeed, charming, but somehow stiff. And gradually I realized he was like the British in another way, too, in that this stiffness came from a kind of emotional over-control. His feelings were there but buttoned up inside him. And then

96

sometimes they would burst out and then, somehow, it was rather nasty.

'One day they burst out with me and I was really quite frightened. I thought he might, well, do something to me. And after that I never felt truly confident with him. I was glad when he suddenly seemed to lose interest in me.

'But the strange thing was that somehow it seemed to have started with Cunningham. One day he seemed to wake up and suddenly hate him. And yet they had been so close! They did everything together. Not just that. You had the feeling that Selim wouldn't do it, or couldn't do it, unless Cunningham did it first. I sort of felt that if Cunningham hadn't been my lover first, then Selim wouldn't, or couldn't have been. It was very strange.

'And then, after having been so close to him, having been like that, he suddenly turned against him. And it was over me! It was as if he had suddenly become jealous.'

'Of Cunningham?'

'Yes. With respect to me. Although there was no need to be, heaven knows. Cunningham didn't care a fig for me. But Selim seemed suddenly to think he did and he didn't like it and it all came exploding out.'

'Perhaps he was jealous of you, not of Cunningham. You say they were very close. Where they lovers?'

'I don't think so. It's sometimes hard to tell in Turkey – young men put their arms around each other, that sort of thing, but that doesn't necessarily mean . . . But I don't think Cunningham was that way inclined, not strongly, anyway. Selim? Well, perhaps. He was always so buttoned-up that it was hard to make him out. I thought at the time that perhaps it was because he was royal. You know, he was used to being the centre of attention and maybe thought I was distracting Cunningham's attention from him. Anyway, he was very nasty to me.

'And I didn't thank Cunningham for getting me into it. And when I thought about it, I thought that he had done it deliberately. You know, had some game of his own and was just using me as a pawn in it. I didn't like that. It seemed so calculating. I am, as I told you, very romantic. I like men to love me for myself, even if it's only for a moment. And Cunningham was not very romantic at all. Even if he did want to swim the Dardanelles like Leander.'

Chapter Seven

Mystery at the Embassy the next morning: Mohammed, the porter-boatman, was not in his usual cubby-hole.

'Damn the fellow!' said Ponsonby, fretting. 'I wanted him to take something for me. Where the hell is he?'

Further investigation cast no light. The Chief Dragoman's aid was enlisted.

'Damn the fellow!' said the Chief Dragoman. 'Where he got to? Disappear up own ass, like Indian Rope Trick?'

The building was scoured but Mohammed did not appear to be in it. Nor, it gradually emerged, had he been in it the previous day. At least, no one had seen him.

'Perhaps he's ill?' said Ponsonby.

'Perhaps he drown,' said the Chief Dragoman hopefully. 'Swim across like Cunningham Effendi. Glug-glug.'

'Someone ought to check,' said Ponsonby.

That someone was clearly the Chief Dragoman. Equally clearly, he had no intention of descending into the town himself. Some minion had to be sent. Enquiry suggested that the most appropriate minion was Ibrahim, the landau driver, perhaps on one of his errands into the city. He, after all, was the man who knew the family. Or, at least, he knew Mohammed's wife's sister-in-law's cousin, which in Istanbul amounted to much the same thing. Ibrahim was therefore instructed to look Mohammed up.

He came back perturbed.

'Effendi,' he said to Ponsonby, 'I don't like this business.'

'Did you find him?'

'Oh, yes, Effendi.'

'Ill, is he?'

'In a manner of speaking,' said Ibrahim mysteriously.

Mohammed, it seemed, was frightened to go out.

'Frightened!' said Ponsonby. 'What's he frightened of?'

'The Fleshmakers,' said Ibrahim unwillingly.

'For Christ's sake!' said Ponsonby. 'You go back and tell him –'

But Ibrahim, it transpired, wasn't at all anxious to tell him anything. In fact, he wasn't willing even to go to his house. Ibrahim, it soon became clear, was as frightened as Mohammed was.

'Damn it!' said Ponsonby. 'We can't have this!'

He decided he would go down to see Mohammed himself. That meant Ibrahim had to drive him. Ibrahim pleaded sickness; malaria, he thought, or dysentery, or – perhaps desperately – typhoid fever.

'You can take us down to the bridge,' said Ponsonby, 'and we'll walk from there. We'll risk the typhoid fever.'

Seymour had asked to go with him.

Ibrahim took them down to the Galata Bridge and gave directions to the street where Mohammed lived. It was in one of the poorer parts of the city and as they drew closer they became aware of an all-pervading smell, a sort of rancid fetidness.

'The tanneries,' said Ponsonby.

It was a whole district and carts piled high with skins and fleeces were coming and going continuously. In the big drying and tanning barns, steamy with heat and thick with flies, men were working stripped to the waist, their arms and torsos mottled with blood.

About them were stacked skins in mounds up to thirty feet high and the ground was littered with little pieces of flesh. Everywhere there were heaps of discarded fleece. The heaps, oddly, were beautifully coloured, delicately tinged with copper and bronze by the processing. The sky was dark overhead with hawks circling, and every now and then one would dart down, pounce on some meat and then fly away again. And everywhere there were dogs scavenging, tearing at the meat and snarling at interlopers, human or canine.

It was an awful place and they hurried through it and into the little streets beyond. The stench was just as great and the flies just as many. They settled on the faces of the children playing in the road and the children did not bother to wipe them away.

Ponsonby frowned.

'I would have thought he could have done better than this,' he said. 'We pay higher wages than most people.'

One reason, perhaps, why Mohammed couldn't live better became apparent when they reached his house. It was full of children. They spilled out into the road, a narrow alleyway strewn with rotting vegetables and smelling like the tanneries.

The door was open and there was a woman inside. She wasn't wearing a veil and when she saw them she tried to shut the door on them. Ponsonby wedged his foot in the door and stopped it from closing.

'Mohammed,' he called out. 'It's Ponsonby Effendi!'

After a long moment, a quavery voice responded from inside.

'It's all right, Mohammed. It's Ponsonby Effendi. No one is going to harm you.'

There was an exchange of words between the man inside and the woman, and then the woman allowed them in. There seemed to be just one room. It was very dark but when his eyes grew accustomed, Seymour could see that a man was in a corner, lying on a mattress.

Ponsonby went across and squatted down beside him.

'What is it, Mohammed?' he said, with surprising kindness.

They began to talk in Arabic, which Seymour could only occasionally follow.

At first Mohammed seemed barely able to speak, but gradually his story emerged. What Seymour didn't gather then, Ponsonby explained to him later.

Two nights before, said Mohammed, as he was making

101

his way home, he had been suddenly seized by some men. One, or perhaps it was two, had held his arms and another had grasped him by the hair and pulled his head back. They had held a knife to his throat and asked him if he was a faithful servant of God and the Sultan. He had, of course, gasped that he was.

'Why, then, do you aid the infidel and the Sultan's enemies?' they had asked.

'I but stand at the door,' Mohammed had protested.

'You do more than that,' they had said, and referred to his rowing the boat across for Cunningham. Mohammed had not known what to say except that the Effendi had bidden it and he was but a poor man, etc.

'You are an enemy of the Sultan and you must die,' the man had said.

Racking his brain in his extremity, Mohammed recalled that some years before his father had done someone in the Sultan's household a service, and he pleaded for this to be taken into account. The men had seemed for the moment taken aback.

'From this you see that I am loyal,' Mohammed had said, pressing home his advantage. 'If I have done wrong, I am but foolish.'

The men had conferred.

'Are you sure that it was Bebek that this service was done for?' they had said threateningly.

'As sure as I am that your knife is at my throat,' Mohammed had said.

'It was his father that did the service, not him,' one of the men had said.

'Yet, for his father's sake, Bebek would surely not wish that we kill him,' someone else had said.

They had conferred some more and then had released him.

'For your father's sake we will let you go,' they said. 'For his loyalty not yours. Learn from him.'

'I will,' Mohammed had promised, no doubt with fervency. 'Oh, I will!'

'Have nothing to do with the infidels! Shun their filthy ways! Lead an upright life!'

'Oh, I will, I will!'

'Tell no man what has happened to you. And this above all: tell no man what happened to you on that other day, the day the mad Effendi was shot.'

Mohammed had muttered that the terjiman and the kaimakam had already asked him questions.

They had seemed to accept that.

'It may be, though,' they had said, 'that they will come again and ask you more questions. And that others will come, too. Say no more. No matter what they ask. Neither about what happened before, nor about what happened after. Nothing! Do you understand that?'

'It would have been better to have killed him,' one of the men had said.

'Bebek would not have liked it. This is a better way to buy his silence,' said the man who seemed to be their leader, 'provided that he understands. You understand, do you?' he had said, turning to Mohammed.

'As God is my witness –'

'He is your witness. And if you break your word, He will know, and so will we. Remember, not a word: neither about the before nor about the after. Be dumb, or else there is for you the long silence.'

Then they had left him. Mohammed had managed to stagger home before collapsing. Since then he had lain on his bed thinking. He liked his job at the Embassy, he told Ponsonby, and he needed the money it had brought in. But, as he said, he also liked his life, and feared that he would lose it if he did not do as the man had said.

'Take no heed of them,' Ponsonby said. 'They are but bandits. You can stay in the Embassy till all is forgotten.'

But Mohammed said that the men were not but bandits. They had not sought to rob him. And they had spoken of the Sultan, and bidden Mohammed to lead an upright life. 'It may be,' he said, 'that they are just men and true servants of the Sultan.'

103

'How can they be just men and true servants of the Sultan when they seize you and threaten you and, if what you say is true, would even kill you?'

'Just but severe,' Mohammed insisted.

It was then that he ventured to name what had so frightened Ibrahim when he had pronounced it to him earlier.

'People speak of the Fleshmakers,' he said.

When they got back to the Embassy Ponsonby went straight in to report to the Ambassador: and about half an hour later he came out and asked Seymour to join them.

The Old Man looked at him over the top of his spectacles.

'Well, Seymour,' he said, 'what, as a policeman, would you say?'

'I would say that someone was trying to frighten witnesses.'

'And why would they do that?'

Seymour hesitated. 'They obviously think the witnesses can tell us something.'

'It is hard to think what,' said Ponsonby. 'I mean . . . Mohammed! What more could he have to tell?'

'I know. Nevertheless, they are obviously worried that there *is* something.'

'Even if, as I gather, he didn't see the actual shooting.'

'They seemed to me to emphasize the before and after. I shall have to look at those again.'

'Please do so . . . And, if you could, before Lady Cunningham gets here!'

'Meanwhile, what are we going to do about Mohammed?' asked Ponsonby. 'I told him he could stay in the Embassy.'

'Well, he certainly could.'

'And his eight children?'

The Ambassador winced.

'I suppose, at a pinch –'

'I am not sure he would want to,' said Seymour. 'He might feel it was less dangerous simply to stay at home. He would be doing what they asked.'

'We could go on paying him, I suppose. A sort of sick leave allowance.'

'If we did that,' said Ponsonby, 'I wouldn't like it to be generally known. Otherwise we'll have all the staff wanting to stay at home and be paid one.'

'But if it was just Mohammed, that could be managed, couldn't it?'

'I suppose it could. Would you like me to see to it, sir?'

'Please.' The Ambassador thought. 'It's a little like giving in, though, isn't it?'

'It's only for a time. Until Seymour completes his investigations.'

'Hmm, yes,' said the Ambassador doubtfully.

'There is one thing,' said Seymour, 'that I think we ought to pursue. This man Bebek.'

'Hmm,' said the Ambassador, even more doubtfully.

'Bebek is a senior official at the court,' said Ponsonby.

'His name was actually mentioned.'

'Yes, but . . . they didn't actually say that he had had anything to do with the attack. Just that he wouldn't like it if things were carried too far.'

'It might be worth talking to him.'

'Well, yes, but it might also be counter-productive,' said Ponsonby.

'Delicate,' said the Ambassador. 'It's always delicate with the court.'

'And what would you ask him? Why they mentioned his name? Because Mohammed had mentioned it first, he would say. In connection with his father! Would you get anywhere?'

'Nevertheless –'

'If there was anything else,' said the Old Man, 'that pointed to him –'

'But there isn't!' said Ponsonby.

'Hmm.'

There was a little pause.

'I think we should proceed with caution,' said the Ambassador.

'Of course, sir, I respect your judgement,' said Seymour.

'Hmm,' said the Ambassador. Doubtfully.

He turned to Ponsonby.

'If there was some other way of doing it!' he said. 'More . . . indirectly.'

'Difficult for us to do it,' agreed Ponsonby. 'As an Embassy. Would raise all sorts of questions.'

'And if Mr Seymour . . .'

'Part of the Embassy, sir, from their point of view.'

'Hmm.'

Pause.

'Someone else, then?'

'But who, sir?'

'This fellow, Mukhtar, perhaps?'

Seymour didn't know much about international relations but he could see plenty of questions about this one.

'Well, that *is* a possibility, sir,' said Ponsonby.

'Seymour seems to get on with him. Perhaps he could . . .'

'Informally,' said Ponsonby.

'These things are often better handled informally.'

'It is, after all, an attack on Embassy staff.'

'Got to do something,' said the Ambassador. 'Lady C. . . .'

'But must keep it in proportion. Not too little. But not too big.'

'An informal word . . .'

'Just so, sir. These things are really quite . . .'

'Delicate,' said the Ambassador.

Hmm.

*   *   *

Seymour took a chance and went to the theatre. Fortunately, Mukhtar was there.

A word?

Certainly.

'I don't want to take you from your work,' apologized Seymour.

'You won't be.'

He led Seymour to a coffee house nearby.

'It's the one the actors go to,' he said, 'and there are some questions I can ask while I'm here.'

'How are you getting on?' asked Seymour.

'Slowly. I have had to work through everybody, you see. It could, in principle, have been anyone working here.'

'An inside job, you mean?'

The terjiman nodded.

'I think so. The players had been rehearsing. They had all been onstage. The others still were. Miss Kassim had come off to change her costume. She was the only one in the dressing rooms at the time. But, of course, only the people involved with the production knew she was there. At that time and in that place.

'Now, of course, it could have been someone who had come in casually off the street. But that is unlikely. The room in which she was changing was at the end of the corridor in a complex of other small rooms and there's a porter at the outside door. You would not, I think, wander there by chance. And if you were coming in from outside and looking for her, the chance of you finding her there and at that moment, well . . .! No, I am proceeding on the assumption that it was someone who worked in the theatre.

'So far I have been going through them. Everybody. Looking largely at time and place. Eliminating where I can. It ought to be easy since everyone here has to be in their place, either up onstage or to do with what's up onstage, and if they're not, the manager goes berserk.

'But in fact it is surprisingly difficult. Yes, people should be in their places, but often they are coming from them or going to them. There is a lot of movement in the theatre and there are frequent changes.

'But, of course, in the end it should be possible. It is just a question of working patiently through. And that is what I am doing.' He smiled. 'Even coming here –' he looked round the coffee house – 'to check on whether they actually were here when they said they were.'

Seymour, interested professionally, nodded agreement. In these circumstances it probably would be just a question of working patiently through.

A thought struck him.

'You will want to check people who have left recently, too,' he said. 'People who worked here once and then left.'

'That is true,' said Mukhtar. 'I shall have to do that.'

Seymour told him about the saz player.

'Saz player?' said Mukhtar. 'I did not know that.'

'He was dismissed. That could be a motive.'

'And,' said Mukhtar, 'the saz is a stringed instrument!'

Seymour told the terjiman about the attack on Mohammed. Mukhtar listened with great attention.

'There could be no question of possible identification, could there?' he said. 'Could he have seen someone? On the beach, perhaps?'

'We've asked him this, and he's said no. And the kaimakam made enquiries –'

'Ah,' said Mukhtar, 'but I've been back since. I went to Abidé. I wanted to talk to the small boys who appeared on the beach afterwards. Well, I found them, and two of them said they *had* seen someone.'

He looked at Seymour.

'A woman,' he said.

'A woman?'

'Yes. At first I thought that that was just a figment of Cunningham's romantic imagination, part of the beguiling story that he had been putting around. But the two boys were definite. They *had* seen a woman. She was climbing up from the beach. They thought that perhaps she had been looking for driftwood.'

'Woman?' said Seymour. He told Mukhtar about the enquiries he had been making.

'Fruitless,' he said. 'This is the first confirmed indication that there was one.'

'I checked at the village nearby,' Mukhtar said, 'the one the children came from. It is some way inland. The women there deny it. They would, of course. But I think they were speaking the truth. No one from the village, they said. Another village, then? But the nearest one is some way away and they were adamant that if someone had come, they would have known.'

He shrugged.

'My enquiries were thorough,' he said, 'but perhaps, in the light of what you say about the attack on the boatman, I should make them again.'

'There is another thing,' said Seymour. 'What about this Bebek who was mentioned?'

The terjiman was silent.

'That is difficult,' he said, after a moment. 'Bebek is a very important person. He is high up at court. One does not go to him and ask questions just like that. Not if one is . . .' he smiled a little ruefully, 'just a simple terjiman. I could, of course, approach my superiors. But they . . .' He shook his head. 'I will have to think about it.'

This was probably as far as he could go. Seymour sensed layers of, probably bureaucratic, complexity. But he could see that Mukhtar was thinking about it and he thought he had detected in him a considerable determination. The terjiman, he thought, would not let go.

Well, Seymour had done what they had asked him to; and now, as the afternoon wore on into evening, he could give his mind to more important things.

Like meeting Felicity.

* * *

They had arranged to meet at the Sultanakhmet Mosque but when he arrived she wasn't yet there and he waited outside.

High above, on the little balconies of the minarets, the muezzins were calling the faithful to prayer. They walked round the balconies, stopping periodically to lean over and call, cupping their hands to make a megaphone. Their voices reached out over the city.

People were beginning to go in. At the big fountain and the taps in the courtyard men were rolling up their trousers and washing their feet before praying.

Felicity touched him on the shoulder and pointed up at the minarets.

'Count them; there are six. That's unusual. There are normally only two or four but the Sultans wanted this to be special. But then it was pointed out that the shrine of the Ka'aba in Mecca had only six and that to have six here was presumptuous. The Sultan had to pay for another one to be added in Mecca.'

There was still some time to go before prayers actually started so they went in, leaving their shoes with the doorkeeper and slipping their feet into big leather slippers provided for the use of infidels.

There were no pews or benches. One prayed on the ground, on the magnificent carpets spread over rush matting. They seemed to stretch away for acres. Men were already coming in and finding their spots. As they did so they bowed to the ground. Over to the left, in a separate enclosure, were the women, bowed black humps.

Felicity pointed to the great dome above covered with the blue tiles that gave the mosque its familiar name. In the darkness they gave off a luminous blue glow.

'Some people don't like them,' whispered Felicity, 'but if you keep looking at them they sort of grow on you.'

Seymour kept looking. After a while the blue glow seemed all around him. So, too, unfortunately, despite the washing, was the smell of feet.

An elderly man came up and tapped Felicity angrily on

110

the arm. He gestured towards the women's enclosure. Felicity half made to go there but then changed her mind and left the mosque.

'They don't usually mind,' she said, when they got outside, 'not if you've got your head and face covered. That man must be one of the more conservative ones.'

They went back afterwards to Felicity's apartment. She boarded in a pension on the lower slopes of Pera Hill, between the Pera and the Grande Rue. It was a district through which Seymour had passed regularly on his descents from the Embassy and he had never given it much attention, beyond noting that it was a poor part of town, with low, wooden houses, narrow cobbled streets full of refuse and dogs, and full, too, of children. He had not expected to find a place in it like the pension.

It was set back off the road in a small, quaint, old-fashioned courtyard, with a surprisingly ornate fountain set in a kind of little house, all intricate stonework, and with a low wall round it, on which, said Felicity, people rested their buckets. All the houses round the courtyard had balconies and vines grew over them and hung thickly to the ground. On one of them a woman was standing, a Greek woman, dressed in black but with her face free, looking out over the courtyard sombrely like some Medea.

She waved to Felicity and Felicity waved back.

'Madame Tsakatellis,' she said. 'She looks after me like a mother. A Greek mother, rather strict. But, somehow, out here I don't mind that.'

Felicity had an apartment on the first floor which gave on to one of the balconies and later in the evening Seymour went out on to it and looked down into the courtyard. The moon had come out and in the courtyard it was as bright as day. The fountain seemed almost silvery.

As he looked at it, something moved behind it. It didn't move again and Seymour was puzzled. He stepped back into the shadow so that he would not be seen, and after a while there was a movement again behind the fountain. A figure came out from behind it and stood for a moment. Then it moved away.

Seymour went back into the room. He didn't know whether to speak of it to Felicity; however he did.

Felicity was matter-of-fact.

'Probably a man having a pee,' she said.

However, she promised she would speak of it to Madame Tsakatellis.

'It's the balcony,' he said. 'I'm a policeman and policeman notice such things. If someone wanted to, they could get in.'

'I've been here for over two years,' said Felicity, 'and I've always felt safe. And I like the balcony.'

'Yes, I know, but –'

He was going to say that Cunningham and Lalagé Kassim had probably felt safe, too, but stopped himself.

'Things might be changing.' he said.

'And in any case I've got a gun,' said Felicity. 'Peter gave it me.'

She fetched it and showed it to him. It was a small revolver.

'Did he show you how to use it, too?'

'Oh, yes. Besides, we Singleton-Mainwarings are used to guns. We handle them from the cradle. Usually shotguns, of course.'

'Yeah, yeah, all right.'

He went out on to the balcony again and looked down. The courtyard was empty and still.

Felicity came out and stood beside him.

'It's true,' she said, 'that things are changing. At least, Peter thought so. I think that, maybe, is why he gave me the gun. He said that the Ottomans were coming to an end, and that might be a good thing because a lot of things needed to be done. The trouble was that when change started to happen, it might not be possible to control it. It would probably crack, he said, along old faults. The old

112

tensions would come again, Greeks versus Turks. Turks versus everybody.

'He said that to Madame Tsakatellis, too. I heard them talking one day. "You think you're safe," he said, "just because you've been here for a long time. But a lot of things are buried in Istanbul and one day the graves will open.

'"You never get rid of the past. No war ever ends, and the Greeks will always be fighting the Turks and the Christians will always be launching Crusades. Those who know no history are doomed to repeat it."

'Well, I was quite impressed. I'd never heard him talk like that before. So seriously. But, of course, you could never trust Peter. The next moment he looked at me and winked.

'"Mind you," he said, "it can work the other way, too. If you know history, you can use it. That's why I'm swimming the Dardanelles."'

Chapter Eight

The next morning, early, Felicity took him to Abydos, or Abidé, as Mohammed, the porter, had called it, the town from which Leander had allegedly set out to swim the Straits to Hero on the other side. Only it wasn't a town now but just some mounds and ruins, in which a donkey was grazing, pulling at the weeds growing in the broken walls. Its owner was hoeing a patch between the mounds and he told them that the nearest village, the one from which the small boys had come to vex Mohammed, was further inland, about a couple of miles away but nearer the beach where Cunningham had landed.

As they drew nearer to it, the stony ground became stony fields, recognizable not by their green or by things growing but by the neatly hoed patches where things might grow. Beyond the fields they could see the houses. They were built out of stone but plastered with mud and had flat roofs on which there were piles of brushwood and onions drying in the sun. Dogs were lying in the shade of the walls, their tongues lolling out.

In the middle of the village there was a well, around which some women were chatting, while one of them lowered a bucket. Further along the street was a café, where men were playing backgammon on marble-topped tables.

It was then that Felicity had an idea.

'Why,' she said, 'don't you leave it to me?'

As soon as she had said it, Seymour knew that she was

114

right. Woman could talk to woman about woman; man couldn't.

'You go to the café,' she said.

The men looked up as he arrived; not just a stranger but a foreign stranger. They were engrossed in their games, however, and, after a cursory glance, returned to their play. He chose a table and sat down.

The front of the café was open to the street and the ground before it was littered with melon-rinds dotted with black flies. The flies were inside the café too, covering the tables. The men disregarded them. At first Seymour was troubled by their constant irritation but gradually, as he settled, they settled, too, and both flies and Seymour became somnolent in the overbearing heat.

The owner of the café brought him tea and a carafe of water. Seymour had asked Felicity about the water but she said that the water in Turkish villages was usually all right.

He could see Felicity now, talking to the women around the well. After a while, she went away with two of them.

A man came into the café and stood at the counter talking to the owner. Seymour suddenly realized that he knew him. It was the kaimakam, Mr – what was it Mukhtar had called him? – Evliya.

The kaimakam recognized him at the same moment and came across to his table.

'Why, Effendi,' he said, 'what brings you here?'

'Just looking around,' said Seymour, 'and hoping to talk to some small boys.'

The kaimakam laughed.

'The terjiman has already done that,' he said.

'So he told me.'

'Was there anything you particularly wanted to know?'

He spoke quite good English. Although when Seymour and Ponsonby had gone to the mutaserrif's house in Gelibolu, the talking had been left to Mukhtar, Seymour had been right in assuming that the kaimakam and the mutaserrif spoke English more than they had revealed.

'I'd like to hear their account of what happened that night.'

'Easy!'

The kaimakam snapped his fingers and a boy appeared. Evliya said something to him and he went off. Shortly after he returned with two other small boys.

Seymour had to put his questions through someone else, which was always unsatisfactory. He was beginning, though, to be able to follow conversation a little, and the clearness of the boys' voices made it easier.

They had been playing and they had heard the shot. They had heard shots before – the soldiers sometimes exercised nearby – and had wondered what this was. When they had got to the top of the cliff they had seen the man lying. The water was all red. One sanguinary touch led to another and other details followed which owed more to imagination than observation. The kaimakam grimaced and spoke to them sternly. They merely gazed at him round-eyed and innocent.

'Was there anything else you wanted to know?' asked the kaimakam, perspiring.

'Yes,' said Seymour. 'There was mention of a woman.'

'A woman?' said the kaimakam, puzzled.

'So Mukhtar said.'

The kaimakam questioned the boys. He seemed dissatisfied with their replies for he questioned them again, disbelievingly. They appeared to be standing by their story. Eventually the kaimakam turned to Seymour.

Yes, he said, they claimed that they *had* seen a woman. After the shooting, some way back on the rocks.

'But these are naughty boys, Effendi. They said –

116

Effendi, I tell you only what they said – they said that she was taking her clothes off.'

'Off?'

'That is what they say. I have told them that they are shameless.'

'Sorry, why would she be taking her clothes off?'

'Effendi, I cannot believe that what they say is true. And it is a shameless thing to say. Or even to think. I shall speak to their fathers.'

'She took her clothes off? But then she would have been –'

'Exactly, Effendi!'

'But –'

'It cannot be true, Effendi. No woman in the village would be so shameless.'

'But then – what did she do next?'

'She went behind some rocks and they lost sight of her. They ran, but by the time they had got to a suitable position to see, she was no longer there.'

One of the boys said something. The kaimakam clipped his ear.

'Effendi, he says that they thought that perhaps there was a man behind the rocks and that she had gone to see him –'

There was a roar of shock and protest from the puritanical backgammon players. The kaimakam tried to clip ears again but the boys scuttled and ran off behind the houses.

'I am sorry, Effendi, I would not have wished you to hear such things! The young, these days, are shameless.'

Mortified at this exposure of the state of the nation, the kaimakam waved to the patron, who brought them some more tea. The tea, milkless, which was the way Seymour preferred it, and was probably safer anyway in Turkey, was amber in its tall glass. In front of the café the sunlight

117

wobbled slightly in the intense heat. From the marble tables inside came the constant click of backgammon counters. The sweat ran down Seymour's bare forearms and gathered beneath his wrists in little pools which evaporated almost as soon as they were formed.

Seymour, as one policeman to another, asked the kaimakam about his work. It was, said the kaimakam, pretty peaceful here. There were boys and dogs to chase and the occasional case of a drunkard to extricate and pilot home but rarely anything more serious; and then it was usually the terjiman who handled it.

Seymour said that he seemed fortunate in his terjiman, and the kaimakam agreed. Mukhtar was a pleasant fellow and chased you around only when it was necessary. Not only that, he did most of the work himself, which was not the usual way with terjimans. But then, Mukhtar was not the usual sort of terjiman.

'Bright,' said the kaimakam, tapping his head significantly. 'Very bright.'

And what he was doing in a vilayet like Gelibolu, the kaimakam could not understand. He had come only six months ago and had at once busied himself with the general organization of the place, going into things that no previous terjiman had ever done. And the kaimakam had to admit that he had not just looked at them, he had done something about them, and usually for the better. Mukhtar was one of those modernizers. The kaimakam did not always hold with people like that, they were more trouble than they were worth. Besides, Gelibolu was hardly the place where change was needed. Let sleeping dogs lie, was the way he looked at it; and, reflected Seymour, glancing up the street there were plenty of sleeping dogs around.

No, Mukhtar was out of place in a vilayet like this one, and the kaimakam didn't expect him to stay long. He hadn't been at all surprised when the vali had sent him over to Istanbul to do whatever it was that he was doing there. Mukhtar was an Istanbul sort of man, and, with his

118

contacts with the army, there was, no doubt, a great future ahead of him.

At the end of the street Seymour saw Felicity. He finished his glass, thanked the kaimakam politely, and said that he must be going. It had been of great interest to him to hear about how colleagues in another country did things and he was most grateful to the kaimakam for his help.

He joined Felicity and they walked back to the beach where she had moored her boat, and Felicity told how she had got on.

One of the women that Felicity had gone off with had been the wife of the local mudir, the village headman. She had taken her to her home and offered her, as people usually did in Turkey, said Felicity, tea and cakes. The house had been rather a good one and she had been interested to see inside. It was bigger than most of the ones in the village and, like most big houses of the well-to-do, had been divided into two parts, the salaamlik, where visitors were received, and the haremlik, where the women lived. Felicity had thought she might be taken into the salaamlik, as a superior visitor, despite being a woman, and had been pleased that she had been shown into the more intimate haremlik.

There had been several small children there and that had given her the opportunity to ask about bigger ones and lead on to the boys who had gone to the boatman's aid. The mudir's own son had, in fact, been one of them and he had come back and told the family all about it, in great and gory detail. The wife had been sorry for the dead man, in a country far from his own and from his own family. Who was there here to carry out the rites? She had spoken about this to her husband, but he had said that the man no doubt had friends in the big city, and was probably a Christian, anyway, and that all that was best left to the mutaserrif and none of her business. All the same, she had felt sad, especially when she had seen the body on the donkey, for

119

the kaimakam had called on her husband to provide the donkey.

The terjiman had brought the donkey back the next day, which was good of him and not the sort of thing that terjimans normally did. This terjiman, though, was very polite and had asked after her children. Her husband had said, though, that the terjiman was not to be trusted, for he had refused the palm-oil when the mudir had gone to him about the road.

Palm-oil? Road?

It was customary, said Felicity, to pay the terjiman some palm-oil if you wanted something done. The terjiman would then bide his time and seize the right moment to approach the mutaserrif or vali. That was how things were done in the Ottoman Empire, by intercession and favour, and for favour something had to be paid. But this terjiman had refused to be paid! So the mudir had known there was something wrong with him.

Road?

Roads were pretty important in Turkey and roads, like favours, had to be paid for. And who paid for them? The villagers, said Felicity, and on a per-head basis, so that everyone paid equally and a disproportionate burden fell on the poorest. Not surprisingly, the 'yol parrasi', the levy for the upkeep and building of roads, was extremely unpopular, particularly as, said Felicity, much of it was, in local phraseology, 'eaten', that is, it was believed to go into the pocket of some official rather than being applied for its proper purpose.

And now here was another thing: the vali had proposed to build a new road just inland from the village. The mudir had, in time-honoured way, sought to have the road diverted so that the village would not have to pay for it, and had offered good palm-oil for that purpose.

But the terjiman had turned it down! Not only that; he had said that the road could not be diverted, that it was necessary for some new works the Government was planning, and that it had to be exactly where the planners had put it.

There had been much muttering among the villagers. Indeed, men had said the road would be built over their dead bodies, and had told the terjiman so. 'So be it,' the terjiman had said, in an unpleasantly steely way, and the mutters had subsided. He had explained that the road was for the benefit of all and would lead, among other things, to greater prosperity for the village. 'We'll believe that when we see it,' the mudir had said to his wife.

Felicity had said that the ways of the mighty were hard to fathom, and that she had a friend who knew the terjiman, and he had told her that he was a nice man; so perhaps he was just doing his duty. The mudir's wife said that she had made the very same point to her husband, but that he had replied, 'Why does the one in our vilayet have to be different from all the others?'

Felicity had sought to divert attention by going back to the original object of her enquiries, the small boys and the shooting. Was it true, she asked, that some women had been involved? For such had been the reports.

If such had been the reports, retorted the mudir's wife hotly, then those who had made them should be ashamed. The women of the village had discussed it among themselves and could swear to it that none of them had been anywhere near the place at the time; and if not them, what other woman could it be, in a place as remote as this? No, the reports were baseless and a malicious fabrication.

And what, asked Seymour, about the boys' claim that they had seen her taking off her clothes?

'Taking off her clothes?' said Felicity, staggered.

Back at the Embassy, over small neatly cut cucumber sandwiches and tea which did not taste quite the same as that brewed in the Whitechapel police station, with the sun glinting less blindingly now on the sea so far below him, and the scent of roses, more powerful, it seemed, in the late

121

afternoon, drifting across the carefully kept grass towards him, with the memory of a relaxed afternoon sail and of a Felicity growing less and less puddingy by the minute, Seymour thought that he could get used to this. If only the tigerish Lady C. was not coming.

Even the difficult Chalmers, sitting by himself on the other side of the terrace, benignly surveying the bougainvillea, seemed at ease with the world, no longer entertaining his private visions of Armageddon. Catching Seymour's eye, he raised his cup to him.

'How are things going, old boy?' he called.

'Oh, fine, thanks. Fine!'

A thought struck him.

'What do you make of this road they're planning to build up behind Gelibolu?'

'Already started building it, old boy. Keeping my eye on it.'

'It will make a difference to the villages, I expect.'

'That's hardly the point, though, is it?' said the military attaché.

'Isn't it?'

'Of course not. It will be to connect the new gun emplacement that they're building.'

'Christ, there he goes again!' Seymour heard Ponsonby mutter beneath his breath.

Seymour dropped into a chair beside Rice-Cholmondely.

'I wonder if I can tap your knowledge of the local scene?'

'Certainly, old boy. Anything I can tell you.'

'Particularly the political local scene.'

'Well, Ponsonby's the chap for that, really . . .'

'Or maybe it's not political but social. Can you tell me something about Prince Selim?'

'Selim? Know him well. A good chap, from our point of view. Almost one of us. Went to a decent school, spent a year at Cambridge, then a couple in Berlin. Talks like us, thinks like us, interested in the sort of things that we are.'

'The theatre?'

'Well, yes, but that wasn't what I was thinking of. I mean modern ways of doing things, engineering, railways, that sort of thing. Reform on Western lines. A bit of a playboy, I suppose, but compared with some of the others . . .'

'Others?'

'Other Princes.'

'There are others?'

'Dozens, old boy. It follows from the Sultan having so many wives and concubines.'

'Well, yes, I can see that it might.'

'Selim's the son of the Sultan's second wife and that puts him quite high up in the pecking order. Of course, they're all always jostling for position. Cut-throat business, being a Prince. At least, in Istanbul.'

'I see.'

'It creates difficulties for us, of course, because the situation's always changing and you never quite know who's in and who's out, so you don't know who to work on. You've always got to keep your fingers on the pulse.'

'And Selim's "in"?'

'Jostling, old boy. Jostling. That's what I would say. But doing pretty well. You never quite know, and the Sultan likes to keep it like that. He doesn't want anyone to get too far ahead of the pack. That would be dangerous. For him, I mean.'

'I gather that Cunningham knew Selim quite well?'

'Oh, yes. You get to know people like that if you're a diplomat. It's part of the job. And Peter had known him before, when he was in Berlin. They had struck it off together and then when Selim got home to Istanbul and found that Peter was there, well, they picked it up and carried on from there. They went round together a lot, you know, doing the shows and clubs.'

'Cultivating him?'

'You could say that, old boy, perhaps. But it wasn't just

123

the line of duty. I think they quite liked each other. But you're right, old boy. Selim could be the coming man, and it was important to get on the right side of him.'

'I wonder if it would be possible for me to meet him?'

'I'm not sure about that, old boy,' said Rice-Cholmondely doubtfully. 'I mean, he's a Prince . . .'

And you're just a policeman, thought Seymour.

'What was it exactly that you had in mind?'

'I wanted to ask him a few questions. About Cunningham's swim. He was the one, after all, who took Cunningham there.'

'Well, he might agree,' said Rice-Cholmondely. 'They were friends and he was very cut up about it afterwards. I'll see what I can do.'

Ponsonby came across to him and said there was another letter for him.

'Not from Lady C., I hope,' said Seymour.

'Could be,' said Ponsonby. 'She believes in striking while the iron is hot, and keeps up a pretty high rate of striking!'

It was not from Lady Cunningham, however. It was from someone completely unexpected. Seymour's grandfather. Grandfather usually reckoned to delegate letter-writing. The writing on the envelope, though, was definitely his. Assuming that this denoted a crisis in the family, Seymour tore the envelope open in alarm.

No crisis.

Or, wait a minute, was it?

The letter, written in a mixture of elegant French (Grandfather claimed to have moved, many years before, in Polish polite circles, where, he assured his family, French was always spoken) and uncertain English, said that since Seymour had been gone, his grandfather had been reflecting on what he had said before he left. He had mentioned a Lady Cunningham; could this be, by any chance, the Lady Cunningham he himself had known?

Seymour did not think this at all likely. His family had spent all their lives in the East End; and Lady Cunningham clearly hadn't.

'When I was working,' Grandfather said. Well, that was a long time ago. If ever. Thirty or forty years at least. When his grandfather had escaped from Poland just ahead of the Tsar's police he had worked for a few years as a horse-cab driver. But that had been in the East End, where he was hardly likely to have run into Lady Cunningham –

But wait a minute: might his journeys not have taken him into the West End?

Well, they might. He might even have given Lady C. a lift at some point. But the letter implied a certain familiarity and that, to say the least, was highly unlikely. In class-ridden England? The Polish émigrés had cultivated, it was true, an image of superiority, superiority temporarily cast on hard times. Every Pole you met in the East End, and you met a lot of Poles in the East End, claimed to be a descendant of Polish nobility, and Grandfather had been no different. There was this in support of his claim, that he had served as an officer in the Tsar's army, and you had to be fairly socially superior to be that. However, Seymour had always discounted the claim. If the family had been so superior, why hadn't some of their money spilled across the Channel to help when it was needed?

It was true that Grandfather claimed to have quarrelled with his family. This was distinctly possible, since Grandfather quarrelled with most people. His father had thrown him out, he said. This was quite possible, too: the Tsar had done the same. For good reason, since Grandfather had tried to blow him up. 'Fighting for Poland's independence!' said Grandfather. Poland was part of the Russian Empire at the time and many Poles were restive under the Tsar's authority. But Grandfather was restive under anyone's authority, and what Seymour was inclined to believe was that he had been restive just once too often.

But, yes, he could tell a good tale and he might have told it to a young and impressionable Lady Cunningham who might just, just, have fallen for the allure of a tall, young, romantic rebel. Even if he was a cab-driver.

But what then? Lady Cunningham would certainly have forgotten it, and, probably, just as well. Grandfather, too, had forgotten it up to this point. At least, it was the rare one of his stories that Seymour had not heard before. But now he had remembered and the memory had evidently been so vivid as to prompt him to give some advice to his grandson, which he had never done before.

'Watch out!' he had said; and he had felt the need for emphasis so great as to underline the words three times.

Seymour felt less impressed by this, however, than by his postscript. 'Do not tell your father!' it said. There was a second postscript: 'Nor your mother!' and a third: 'Nor your sister!' Well, Seymour could understand that, as his sister was always difficult. However, taking it altogether, and all in all, Seymour definitely had the feeling that this was part of Grandfather's life description which he thought better suppressed.

As for the warning, Seymour was unmoved. He was just doing his job and doing it as well as he could. More than that he could not do, and he was not at all bothered by the imminent arrival of what was evidently a lively domineering old lady, even if she had put the fear of God into everyone she met.

Including his grandfather. That, admittedly, was a thought.

Chapter Nine

The Prince's boat would pick him up outside the Dolmabahce Palace.

'Boat?'

'He's at his estate at Beylerbey,' explained Rice-Cholmondely.

Beylerbey, it transpired, was on the opposite side of the Bosphorus, more or less straight across from the Dolmabahce, one of a number, said Rice-Cholmondely, of pretty villages. It wasn't far, just far enough to allow the Prince to distance himself from Istanbul when he wished to.

Then a thought struck Seymour.

'Boat? Would that be his felucca?'

'I expect so,' said Rice-Cholmondely offhandedly.

And there, when Seymour got to the Dolmabahce, an hour later, was the felucca, with its distinctive green flag flying, drawn up alongside the long, marble quay.

A splendidly dressed cavass showed him on board and at once the felucca drew away from the quay. There was, apparently, no other passenger aboard.

They moved quickly to the other side and then went along the coast for a little way. The shore was thickly wooded but there were small villages tucked among the trees. The white minarets of their mosques poked out above the green and here and there were other white buildings, deserted kiosques and small, rejected palaces, graceful relics of past Sultans' temporary enthusiasms. The villages, with their wooden houses, sometimes came down to the water's edge, and among the acacia and maple and plane trees he could make out winding, cobbled streets, often with little cafés under the trees.

Beylerbey was like that, a small village, all cool and green, with a single street, at the end of which was the Prince's country palace. They disembarked and the cavass set off up the street.

Ahead of them was an old man in a turban. From time to time he stooped and picked something up, offending litter, perhaps, and pushed it into a cranny of the nearest wall. When they caught up with him Seymour saw that they were pieces of paper. The cavass, shaking his head at this display of rustic backwardness, explained – in perfect French – that it was the custom among the simpler Muslims to pick up any piece of paper that had printing on it, on the grounds that among the writing might be one of the Holy Names, on which it would be disrespectful to tread.

They came to an imposing gate with several resplendent cavass-like figures lounging outside it. Seymour's cavass had a word with them and then told Seymour that the Prince was awaiting him in the garden. For a moment Seymour thought that he was going to be left to find the Prince himself, which might prove tricky as the garden was more like a park, with great plane trees, clumps of shrubbery which shut off any view and hosts of little streams, with bridges, admittedly, but which required crossing. However, one of the subsidiary cavasses came with him to guide him.

The Prince was standing beneath a plane tree looking up into its branches. He had a young man beside him who was carrying a rifle. The Prince pointed up into the foliage and the young man raised his gun and fired. A pigeon came fluttering down. The young man bent over it, picked it up and threw it into a basket.

The Prince saw him and came to meet him.

'Seymour, is it?' he said, in excellent English. They shook hands.

'Do you know Ahmet?' he said, gesturing towards his companion.

Unexpectedly, Seymour did. It was the sulky youth he had seen talking to Mukhtar outside the theatre.

He was still sulky and gave Seymour just a bare nod.

The Prince noticed it and gave a little laugh. He pushed the boy away, in friendly fashion.

'Go and look for a fat one,' he said. 'I want to talk. Or, rather,' he said, looking at Seymour, 'I fancy Mr Seymour does.'

He was dressed in a white suit and silk shirt and tie. The tie was – well, Seymour would have said it was regimental. Chalmers wore a tie like that. There was something army-like in general about the Prince, as if he had been to Sandhurst, although, to the best of Seymour's knowledge, he hadn't. He was certainly very English.

'Well, my dear chap –'

There it was: that British, upper-class way of speaking, the product, presumably, of the schools they all went to, and the lingua franca of the top part of the institution they worked in, the officers in the army, the senior civil servants, the diplomats in the Embassy. The governing class, you might say.

'– how can I help you?'

'It is very kind of you to receive me. As I expect you know, I am out here to investigate Peter Cunningham's death –'

The Prince laid his hand on his sleeve.

'And I am very glad you are,' he said. 'If ever a thing needed investigating, this is it. And for a number of reasons.'

He cleared his throat, as if he were going to make a speech.

'First, obviously – and someone like me has to think of that – because of the effect it could have on relations between Britain and ourselves. Secondly, and I hope you will believe this, because it's true, because my whole family is shocked and ashamed. That something like this

129

could happen to Peter, a man whom we all knew and liked . . .'

He shook his head.

'Let me just say that my father is particularly sad. He is very anxious that whoever did this terrible thing should be brought to justice. But there is a third thing.'

His voice lost its stiffness and formality.

'Peter and I were very close. We met first at university but then ran into each other several times when he was working in Europe. We got to know each other particularly well in Berlin.'

He smiled.

'We even went on holiday together. To Biarritz, I remember.'

He smiled again at the recollection.

'So when I came back to Istanbul and found that he had been posted out here I was delighted. It can be very lonely, you know, if you're someone like me. You get depressed. Well, Peter could always jolly me out of it. He was such good company. And he'd put you on to things you'd never heard of. And they might be here in Istanbul! In my own city, and he knew it better! That's how it is, I'm afraid, if you belong to a family like mine. You're cut off, you don't even know your own people. Well, Peter knew them.'

They had been walking while he spoke and he had unconsciously quickened his pace. By the end they were almost racing along. He suddenly became conscious of this and slowed embarrassedly.

'Sorry, old man, but Peter meant something to me.'

The decent reticence, thought Seymour, was upper-class British, too.

'He was a good chap,' said Selim. 'It's very important to me personally to find out who killed him.'

He half turned away so that Seymour could not see his face.

'I keep telling myself,' he burst out, 'that surely I could have done something. Even, maybe, to put him off the whole crazy idea. I tried, you know, but he made a joke of it, it seemed pompous, elderly, to argue with him.'

He shook his head.

'But I should have, shouldn't I?'

'You were on the other side of the Straits,' Seymour pointed out. 'There was nothing you could have done.'

The Prince was silent.

'Well, no,' he said after a moment. 'Perhaps not. All the same . . .'

'May I ask how it was that you came to be there at all?'

'I suggested it. "Look, old chap," I said, "if that fellow of yours is going to row you there to start with, he's going to be dead beat before you even get to the swimming. I can help you with that. But I'm not – I'm definitely not! – going to do the swim with you. It's foolhardy, old man. And a Prince, even if not a diplomat, has got to show some sense!"'

'Well, it *was* helpful of you,' said Seymour. 'He'd have had to get hold of another boat, somehow or other, to get there. So he would have been glad of your help, I'm sure. And of your company. But there is something that puzzles me. After he had set out, on the swim, I mean, you stayed there for quite some time. You even had a haircut.'

'Damned bad one, too. Well, it was a way of killing the time.'

'Killing the time? You weren't *waiting* for him, were you? Waiting for him to swim back!'

'Good God, no. No, I was going to pick him up. On the other side. So I had to wait until I was sure he'd got there. And it's a hell of a long way. I mean, if you're swimming. So I thought I'd give him plenty of time. Give him a chance of a breather, too, after he'd done it. And, well, I left it a bit late, I suppose. Took longer to get that damned haircut than I had thought.'

'And then did you actually do it?'

'Do what?'

'Go across to the other side?'

'Oh, yes. Knew where he was going to go. Been there with him before. Showed me the place. "Abydos," he said. "It's got to be the right place."'

'But . . .'

'But what?'

'It *wasn't* the right place. The right place was on the other side. Leander swam from Abydos to Sestos. Not from Sestos to Abydos.'

'Well, look, never can remember which is which. But I certainly went back to the place he showed me.'

'And . . .?'

'Well, nobody there! We went right in, came out, went up and down a few times. Thought the current might have taken him, you know. Landed somewhere else. Thought maybe he'd found someone else to give him a lift. Or maybe had walked over to the village -'

'Did you see any sign of a woman?'

'Sorry, old boy?'

'A woman. Over on that side?'

'Look, old boy, it's a hell of a place. I mean, it's not the place you would go to if you were in search -'

'No, no. But a woman was part of the original plan. A Hero for him to swim across to.'

'Don't know anything about that, old boy.'

'And you didn't see anyone else? The boatman, boys, the kaimakam?'

'Not a soul, old boy. Couldn't make it out. Went up and down. Until it was so dark you wouldn't have seen anything even if it had been there. A bit irked, as a matter of fact. Thought he ought to have told me if there'd been a change of plan.'

Ahmet, the boy, had come back and was hovering: not exactly patiently.

'Did you say, old boy, that he ought to have been swimming the other way?'

'Yes. According to the legend.'

The Prince seemed put out.

'Damned strange,' he said.

Ahmet kicked a stone: apparently aimlessly, but ostentatiously. Seymour thought that perhaps it was time to go.

'Well, thank you very much, Prince Selim. What you've told me has been very interesting. And helpful. Although, I must confess, puzzling.'

'Damned right,' said Selim. 'That's what I said. And that's why, I said to them, you need a proper investigation. Western style. Modern. It's not just a case of going out and bastinadoing a few people. You've got to get it properly investigated. But no one listens to me,' he said sadly, 'on a thing like that.'

The boy, restless, went over to one of the large plane trees and peered upward into its branches. Then he put the gun to his shoulder and fired. A bird fell like a stone.

'Good shot!' said the Prince, patting him affectionately on the shoulder. 'Wants to go in the army,' he said to Seymour.

'You promised,' said the youth.

'So I did. We'll have to see about it, won't we? Damned good thing, the army,' he said to Seymour. 'Modern. One of the few things in the Ottoman Empire that works.'

Ahmet picked up the bird and threw it into the basket.

'Hardly worth it, is it?' said the Prince, fishing it out and throwing it away into the bushes. 'No good taking that to the kitchens!'

It was, Seymour, saw, a sparrow.

The cavass spoke French, the captain didn't. Nor did the crew, and it was the people who sailed the boat that he wanted to talk to. Seymour's Turkish and Arabic were coming along – he had been working hard since his arrival – but he knew that wouldn't be good enough. He wished Felicity were with him.

Felicity! There was a thought. And with it came another. Wasn't she supposed to be rehearsing this afternoon with the quartet? She would be at the Embassy.

And, indeed, when he got there, he could hear faint quavery sounds from somewhere in the back.

Eventually, she emerged, hot and bothered and carrying her cello. She went pink when she saw him.

He took her over to the other side of the terrace and put it to her.

'Gosh, yes!' said Felicity. 'Certainly, I could!' Then doubt crept in. 'Do you think I could?'

'I'm sure you could. And, actually, I think you'd be rather good at it.'

'Really?' said Felicity, pleased. 'Do you really think so? Gosh!'

Waiting for him, too, was an invitation from Mukhtar to join him at a musical recital that evening. 'It will be in a private house,' his note said: 'the house of a Mr Cubuklu. Mr Cubuklu is a senior official at the Palace.'

Seymour thought that might be interesting. He feared, though, that the music might be less so. However, he took the landau down to the Galata Bridge at the appointed time and found the terjiman waiting.

'I have found your saz player,' he said, smiling, 'and I thought you would like to hear him.'

He accompanied Mukhtar to an old house in the Sultan-ahmet, not far from the mosque they had visited the day before. It was a beautiful old quarter, full of fine Ottoman houses in the traditional wooden style. Seymour suspected that other things might be traditional, too: plumbing, for instance. At almost every corner there was a well, around which the women of the district gathered, gossiping, their wooden buckets resting on the ground nearby.

The house itself seemed nothing from the street. There was just a high bare wall with a large, very large, wooden door set in it. However, when the door opened, they stepped straight into a small, beautiful courtyard surrounded by arched colonnades at ground level and protruding, boxed, glassless windows above. A flight of steps led up to an enclosed verandah which gave every sign of being much used.

From the verandah they went through into the large room where the recital was to take place. At one end was a low dais on which the performer was to sit. Scattered about the marble floor were huge embroidered cushions on which people were already reclining. There weren't many of them.

'Just a few friends,' said Mr Cubuklu, coming forward and shaking hands with Seymour in the European manner. For Mukhtar there was a quick embrace which Mukhtar went to refuse, as too generous an expression of the host's favour, but was overruled.

Mr Cubuklu was an elderly grey-haired man in the gown traditionally reserved for indoors. He had a more bony face than most Turks and sharp grey eyes. He went to the end of the room and sat down in front of the dais, and, just at that moment, the musician appeared, carrying a weird stringed instrument. He bowed nervously to the audience and twice to Mr Cubuklu and then squatted down.

Seymour hadn't been sure what to expect. Not this, he thought, after the musician had begun playing. It wasn't, of course, European music and had the strange half tones of the music he had heard from the cafés; but there was in addition a kind of dancing, gypsy-like melody. The dance gave way, after some time, it must be said, to a mournful, wailing sort of music, to which, however, the audience listened, rapt.

This, too, continued for quite some time before it gave way to another wailing song, and then another. Then there was another jaunty, dancing piece, like the first, and then attendants came round with plates of sweetmeats.

A man in front of them turned round.

'Most unusual, isn't it?' he said, in French. 'To have a concert of saz music?'

'Most unusual,' Mukhtar agreed. 'But delightful, don't you think?'

'Oh, yes,' said the man.

Someone brought the saz player a glass of water. He sipped at it and then returned to his instrument, caressing it, without once raising his eyes and looking at the audience.

Mr Cubuklu had gone across the room to greet a man who had come in late. Judging by the way Mr Cubuklu received him, he was a man of some consequence.

'Prince Hafiz,' whispered Mukhtar.

Mr Cubuklu escorted the Prince to the front and made a place for him beside him. At once the saz player resumed his playing.

The music was attractive but Seymour was not used to sitting on the floor for hours and after a while found it hard to concentrate. His mind wandered and he fell into a drowse until a change in the music alerted him to the fact that the recital was coming to an end. He looked up and saw that the person of consequence had gone.

The saz player finished and sat bowed in front of the audience. It was with evident relief that he escaped from the applause and went off into an inner room.

'Of course, he's not used to playing in a place like this,' said Mukhtar. 'He's a street musician, really.'

Mr Cubuklu, circulating, stopped in passing.

'Mr Cubuklu, how can I ever thank you?' cried Mukhtar.

'He *is* rather good, isn't he?' said Mr Cubuklu, beaming.

'Remarkable!'

'Quite a discovery. For which we have to thank your colleague,' he said to Seymour.

Colleague?

'When he recommended him to me, I thought: what does an Englishman know of our music? But Cunningham Effendi was an unusual man. Such an ear! And such a sympathy for things Turkish!'

This was a new side of Cunningham, thought Seymour.

'A real discovery! And in an ordinary Istanbul street! Of

136

course, that is where a saz player should be, but it is not everyone who can spot a jewel when it is covered with dust. You've heard about how he came to find him, I expect?' he said, turning to Seymour.

'No? Well, it was an ordinary street near the bazaars. Close to the Place of Scribes. He was passing by when he heard him playing. It was just to an ordinary, disregarding crowd, but he stopped and listened. And he realized at once that he was listening to an extraordinary talent. He told me afterwards that he just stood there, entranced. And when he moved on – because that's what they do, of course, they're genuine street musicians – he went with him. He stayed with him for the whole of that afternoon, he told me.

'By the end of the afternoon, he told me, he knew he had to do something about him, and he took him along to the Theatre of Desires and introduced him to the people there. Afterwards he thought that perhaps that had not been a good idea, but at the time it was the only one he could think of. At least they found him a bed for the night.

'But they wouldn't pay him, did you know that? They said it had to come out of the band's ordinary money, which, of course, didn't help matters. So what Cunningham did was to arrange to go to him for private lessons himself, so that the charge would not fall on the band. Most generous, don't you think? Sadly, though, it didn't work out. It was caviare to the general. So he brought him to me and asked if I could do something to help. And, of course, when I heard him play . . .!'

'You are unjust to yourself, Mr Cubuklu,' said Mukhtar. 'It was very generous to take him under your wing.'

'Well, of course, it's not really my wing. It's more Prince Hafiz's. He was here earlier this evening. I wonder if you saw him? He is a great supporter of such causes.'

'The Prince is an enthusiast for folk music?'

'We share the passion.'

'And it is very kind of you, Mr Cubuklu, to share it with us.'

'It is something I shall take back with me to England,' said Seymour. 'This delightful acquaintance with old Turkey.'

'There is still a little of it left,' said Mr Cubuklu, modestly, but pleased. 'But what there is has to be nourished.'

'Which is what you do so well, Mr Cubuklu. Your protégé is indeed fortunate to have found so good a patron.'

'Ah, yes, but will he stay? These saz players are not like ordinary musicians, you know,' he said to Seymour. 'They are wanderers. Like gypsies. Of course, that is how they find their songs. In small, obscure villages, where a man has been singing them for centuries. But that is what is so good about them, they are the well undefiled. All that comes after . . .'

He shook his head sorrowfully.

'Mr Cubuklu,' said Mukhtar, 'I wonder if I could have a few words with him? Perhaps tomorrow, when he has recovered from this evening? There are some questions I would like to ask him.'

'Questions?'

'In my professional capacity, I'm afraid. I am a terjiman. I shrink from introducing a discordant note after such an evening but they concern the death of an actress at the Theatre of Desires.'

'An actress? But, surely, there are no actresses –'

'And, possibly, that of Cunningham Effendi,' said Mukhtar hurriedly.

'But all this is very unsavoury!' said Mr Cubuklu.

'It is indeed. The law, however, gives us no option, I'm afraid.'

'But the Prince –'

'Need not concern himself in any way. Nor be involved. I wish only to put a few questions to the saz player. They need not take long.'

'They will upset him,' said Mr Cubuklu, changing tack. 'These people are very sensitive.'

138

'I can promise you that I will do all I can to see that he is not upset.'

'I am not sure, however, that I can allow . . . An actress, did you say? Is that really important? Important enough to justify such –'

'And, of course, Cunningham Effendi. Possibly.'

'Cunningham Effendi? Well, of course, that does make a difference. Well . . . Perhaps tomorrow morning, then,' said Mr Cubuklu reluctantly.

'Thank you, Mr Cubuklu. And thank you again for letting me share your pleasure. And, too, for allowing me to bring my friend.'

'It is a great privilege, sir, to be given the opportunity to hear such playing,' said Seymour, shaking hands. 'Even if, as a foreigner, one cannot hope to do it justice.'

Mr Cubuklu nodded approvingly.

'One of the old school,' said Mukhtar enthusiastically, as they walked away. 'You don't meet many like him these days. So civilized, so refined! A real, old-style Ottoman gentleman! I thought you might like to meet one to see how it used to be.'

'Yes, indeed.'

'Of course, I am not an intimate of his, so it was very kind of him to invite us this evening. He is a friend of the father of one of my friends who is interested in music. I mentioned to my friend that I was trying to track down a saz player and he said, well, if it's saz players you want, there is someone you must meet, a Mr Cubuklu. And it turned out that he was precisely the person that Cunningham had taken the saz player to when he was thrown out of the band!'

'It appears that he went on to share him with Prince Hafiz?'

'Well, of course, a Prince can do far more in the way of patronage than a Councillor, even one as senior as Mr Cubuklu. He was doing him a favour. And, of course, he was fortunate that Mr Cubuklu knew someone like Prince Hafiz who is interested in saz music. I mean, that is unusual in Palace circles. The saz is, what shall I say, a lowly instrument. For many in the Palace it would be beneath them. It is only someone like Mr Cubuklu, who treasures old traditions, who would take an interest in it.'

'And, apparently, Prince Hafiz?'

'That is even more unusual. But, then, Hafiz is different from most of the other Princes. They are mostly, well, playboys and layabouts. But Hafiz seems to have a genuine interest in the arts. Certainly the Ottoman arts, particularly the old ones. That is good, it is good that the Royal Family should take an interest in such things. But it is good, too, that he takes an interest in the saz, for the saz is an instrument of the people.'

He smiled.

'You will gather, perhaps, that I am on the side of the people.'

'Well, as a policeman, you should be.'

'Yes, but it is more than that. In our country there is much that needs doing. And under the old Sultan too little has been done.'

He stopped, as if he had said too much, or spoken out of turn.

Chapter Ten

Seymour had arranged to meet Felicity for lunch. The
landau was in use so he went down on foot, which was,
actually, a relief to him. He always felt uncomfortable up
there in the landau. It seemed a needless affectation of
superiority. No landaus in the East End; at least, not for
policemen!

The morning, too, was fresher than of late, with a dis-
tinct, cooling breeze coming up off the Horn, and he rather
enjoyed the walk down; past the cemetery with its mortuary families, past the fruit markets with their fly-spotted
fruit and porters crouched under heavy baskets, their arms
hanging down ape-like, their hands almost brushing the
ground. Past, too, the Theatre of Desires, with stagehands
and workmen squatting on the steps, making the most of
a break, he supposed.

Suddenly, the little theatre manager came rushing out.

'They're after me!' he shouted. 'They're trying to finish
me! They strangle my leading actress, they shoot my script
writer, they try to frighten my people away! They're trying
to drive me out. But they won't! I'll fight back. I'll show
them. Rudi Sussenheim is not the man to be beaten.'

He dashed back inside.

The workmen looked at each other.

'What the hell's he on about?'

'The police are everywhere this morning,' someone
said.

'Yes, but –'

The little man dashed out again, this time pushing the

youth Seymour had seen with Prince Selim the day before.

'Your chance!' he shouted. 'I give you your chance. And do you take it? No, you just loll around. You can't be bothered. The theatre is too hard for you. Acting is too hard for you. Anything is too hard for you! Except lowering your trousers and turning your backside towards some rich man.'

'Raoul hasn't learned his lines,' said the youth.

'Well, does that stop you from saying yours? Say yours and that will help him.'

'He never helps me!'

The little man beat his forehead with his fist.

'Can't you see? This is the time when we all have to work together. Or else we'll be done for! Oh, my God, why am I surrounded by idiots?'

'Raoul is too old. He's past it.'

'It's too late to find someone else. We have to make do. We have to put aside our differences and work together. That is what the theatre *is*. Oh, my God, what has happened to you all when I even have to say such things! But you, you haven't the true spirit of an actor. I found you lying in the gutter –'

'No, you didn't! I came along and –'

'I gave you your chance. And how do you repay me?'

'It's just that you need me now that Lalagé's gone.'

'I was building you up. Getting you ready. I spend months training you, I teach you all I know. I get you ready so that you can do something *big*. And then, when you are ready, when all the world is before you, what do you do? You hang back. You make difficulties. Just when the troupe needs you most. In its hour of need! Look, all I want you to do is stand in for our best actress. That's all! Our best! What a chance I am giving you!'

The youth hesitated.

'Can I wear the red dress?'

'Of *course* you can wear the red dress! It's yours. Think how you will look! Wonderful! Your chance! Glittering!'

'All right, then, but you'll have to speak to Raoul.'

'I *have* spoken to Raoul. Come on, now. We're all waiting for you.'

'Go on your knees!'

'Isn't this going on my knees? Come on. Please!' The little man swallowed. 'I beg of you!'

'All right, Rudi. If you put it like that.'

The youth looked around triumphantly. Then, reluctantly, but only half reluctantly, he allowed himself to be pushed up the steps and inside.

'Asshole!' said one of the workmen.

'A bloody khaval,' said another.

'Bloody gink!' said a third.

The little manager rushed back out.

'Come on, come on!' he said. 'What are you doing?'

'Waiting for the police to get out. They're everywhere this morning.'

'They're not on the stage, are they? Come on, get in there!'

Over lunch, down by the Galata Bridge, Felicity told him how she had got on.

She had gone down to the quay, she said, immediately after he had spoken to her. The Prince's felucca hadn't been there and she had had to wait some time before it drew in. Then, while the crew was polishing the brass, or, possibly, gold, she had managed to strike up a conversation with the captain.

They had talked about the felucca. It was, the captain told her, the apple of the Prince's eye. For the moment; there was a frequent turnover in apples. He made regular use of it to go over to his estate on the other side.

'It's a lovely boat!' said Felicity enthusiastically.

'He wants to put an engine in it,' said the captain grimly.

'Into this beautiful felucca?' cried Felicity, aghast, all her yachtswoman's instincts roused.

143

Her concern and, as obviously soon became apparent, her nautical knowledge, struck chords in the captain's heart. He expanded visibly. Yes, he sailed the Bosphorus and the Sea of Marmara –

'Right up to the Dardanelles?'

To the Dardanelles, yes, and even, on occasion, into the Mediterranean. 'To the Gates of Hell if necessary,' he declared, fired. But that hadn't been necessary so far.

Felicity had mentioned Cunningham's swim.

'That's how it is with the rich,' said the captain. 'One nutty thing after another!'

Yes, he'd taken them over to the Sestos side and watched Cunningham and the porter set out.

'Goodbye, Sinbad!' he had called to the boatman, as the boat departed. 'Tell us about your adventures when you get back. If you get back.'

They had waited on the point for hours. And in the middle, would you believe it, the Prince had gone to get his hair cut! Even when he got back, they had hung on there. Not until the sun was about to go down had Selim agreed to move. And then, instead of going home, as the captain had assumed, they had sailed over to the other side. The captain had thought that they were going to pick up Cunningham and the boat but no, they hadn't gone there at all, he knew the spot, they had been there that morning to look it over. No, they had gone in further along the coast and picked someone else up, who he presumed was a friend of the Prince's.

Had he seen the person? Well, no, it had been dark and the person had been muffled up.

Had it been a woman, asked Felicity?

Woman? No, said the captain, surprised. The suggestion, though, had put other romantic, or, possibly, less romantic ideas in his head and Felicity had been obliged to speak about her warlike military husband and beat a retreat.

The captain had later gone ashore and disappeared into

the Dolmabahce Palace. The moment he had gone, the crew had abandoned its polishing and gone ashore too, to sit upon bollards in the shade and commune with the sea in the way usual among sailors. Felicity had seized the chance to return, apparently casually, and check one or two points in the captain's story.

In particular, she had asked them about the earlier voyage, the one in the morning.

To the Dardanelles twice in one day? That was a bit much, wasn't it?

It certainly was. True, they got paid for it, but not enough, and in their opinion there was more to life than pretty uniforms. However, the Prince had insisted on it, had, indeed, come himself, although he had stayed in the cabin – there was, as you might expect, a small but luxurious cabin on this felucca – and in the shade and not come out until they had reached the bay where they were to set the passenger down.

Just a minute: which bay was this? The one they returned to in the afternoon?

No, no, that hadn't been a bay. Just a point, really. And it had been on the other side, the Sestos side. All rocks, and as hot as hell. And why the Prince should have chosen to tie up there and spend all afternoon . . . Not to mention going off into the desert and getting his hair cut . . .

No, no, this was on the other side, the Abidé side.

'Where the Effendi was supposed to be swimming to,' put in one of the other members of the crew helpfully. He had heard the Prince say that to the captain.

And, just a minute, they had put someone down there?

'That's right.'

One of the crew?

No, no, a passenger. They hadn't known he had been there. He had stayed in the cabin all the time with the Prince. He had come out only when they had actually moored and they had taken him ashore in the dinghy.

Had they seen him? What sort of person was he?

145

'Well . . .'

A woman?

Guffaws.

'Listen, if it had been a woman, Selim wouldn't have been putting her ashore, I can tell you!'

It had been a man, and obviously a friend of Selim's. The Prince had stood there watching him land and then had carried on watching him, though binoculars, until he had disappeared into the cliffs.

And then?

Well, then they had bloody sailed home again, and the moment they got there had turned round and sailed straight back up to the Dardanelles once more, only this time with Cunningham and the crazy old boatman aboard.

Just one other thing: when they were sailing home again, at the end of it all, they had put in again, hadn't they, and picked someone up?

They certainly had.

Had that person been the passenger they had put ashore earlier in the morning?

Yes/no/couldn't see. It had been dark. The person had shone a lamp from the shore. They had been under lamps, too, by this time. Pitch black, it had been. They hadn't really seen the person who had come aboard. Nor had they seen him when he had got off at Istanbul. He had left with the Prince and they had had their heads down because the Prince had told them to get on with it and move their asses.

'Was that what you wanted me to find out?' finished Felicity. 'It doesn't sound very much –'

'It will do fine,' said Seymour.

Oh, said Felicity, and she had received three proposals of marriage and one which was almost certainly not for marriage.

Back at the Embassy later that afternoon, sitting in the

room that had been assigned him, Seymour had been aware of a certain commotion at the end of the corridor. Some time later Ponsonby stuck his head round the door.

'I say, old man, would you mind coming to see the Boss? He's got a bit of a problem.'

Even before he entered the room Seymour could guess the nature of the problem.

'I'm a British national, aren't I?' said Nicole. 'He can't do nuffink to me!'

'Well, yes,' said the Ambassador, 'that's true. Up to a point.'

Nicole regarded him suspiciously.

'I knew there'd be a catch in it,' she said.

'You are obliged to co-operate.'

'I am co-operating, aren't I? 'E's been round all day asking bloody questions and I answer them, don't I? And the last time 'e came, I offered 'im a cup of tea. Isn't that co-operating?'

'Well, it depends how much you tell him. And how readily.'

'I 'aven't got anyfink else *to* tell 'im. 'E's wormed it all out of me.'

'Who is this?' asked Seymour.

'Mukhtar,' said Ponsonby.

'And what have you told him?'

'What 'e asked me. About Babikr. That saz player. 'Ow well did 'e know Lalagé? 'Ow well did *I* know 'im? "Look," I said, "I felt sorry for 'im. That's all." But 'e went on and on.

''Ad 'e been round to the flat? "Look," I said, "we're a troupe. Everyone comes round. Sometimes you want to get away when you've been rehearsing 'ard. You're given ten minutes' break. Well, where do you go? In ten minutes you can't go far. And our place is 'andy. So, yes, people come round: Monique, and Raoul, and Gilbert, and even that little prick, Ahmet. And the band, too, because they rehearse with us. Farraj, and 'Ussein, and bloody 'Assan, who's getting very fed up with all this. So, yes, Babikr, too, although not much, because 'e was so shy and didn't get on with the others."

'And what was 'is relation to Lalagé? "Bloody dirt," I says. "She looked on 'im as bloody dirt." Brushed 'im off, 'e said? "She never brushed 'im on," I told 'im. "Didn't even see 'e was there." Was 'e upset by that? Was there antagonism between them? "Upset?" I said. "Listen, 'e was upset by everything. Antagonism? Look, 'e was as quiet as a mouse. There was nuffink to 'im."

'But he was a member of the band, wasn't 'e? "The band didn't think so," I said. But 'e worked in the theatre? "Well, of course 'e did!" So 'e would 'ave known about the dressing rooms? "What?" I said. 'E would 'ave known about the dressing rooms. Been up there, perhaps? "Listen," I said, "the dressing rooms are for people who *dress*. Actors only, see. And make-up people. You don't 'ave band going up there. Christ, it's not a bloody thoroughfare. We undress, too, you know."

'All right, but 'e would 'ave known where they were, wouldn't 'e? And – and 'e looks at me very sharp – 'e would 'ave known *when* she was there, wouldn't 'e? Presumably, you've got a rehearsal programme?

'"Programme?" I said. "With Rudi? You've got to be joking!" Yes, but 'e would be able to work it out, wouldn't 'e? 'E would know when you were all onstage, and when she was off it? "Work it out?" I said. "Babikr? That poor bastard couldn't work out if 'e 'ad 'is trousers on!" But 'e must 'ave known when 'e wouldn't be playing . . .

'And on and on. All day! It's been bloody terrible down there today, I can tell you. 'E's 'ad everybody in and gone round and round twice. And then 'e picked on me! And that's what I've come to see you about. It's bloody 'arassment it is. And I'm a British national, and I've got my rights –'

'Yes, yes,' said the Ambassador wearily.

'So what are you going to do about it?' asked Nicole suddenly.

'Do about it?'

'I mean, you've got to do somefink about it now, 'aven't you? Now I've made a complaint.'

'Well, yes. I suppose so –'

'Otherwise your bosses back in London will be up your ass, won't they?'

'Well, in a manner of speaking –'

'Is this a formal complaint?' asked Ponsonby.

'What?'

'A formal complaint.'

'Well, I suppose so.'

'Then it has to be in writing.'

'You've got the gist of it, 'aven't you? Can't *you* write it down?'

'Has to be written. To be a formal complaint.'

'Bastards!' said Nicole, looking hunted.

'Look, Miss – Miss – Nichols? – why don't you leave it with us?' said the Ambassador. 'I'll put someone on to it.'

'You'll bloody forget about it,' said Nicole.

'No, I won't!' said the Ambassador, injured. 'I'll get someone on to it right away. Tomorrow.'

'And if you're not satisfied,' said Ponsonby maliciously, 'you can always put a complaint in. In writing, of course.'

'Bastard!' muttered Nicole under her breath.

'Well, thank you very much for calling, Miss Nicholas,' said the Ambassador, holding out his hand. 'Shall I get someone to call your carriage?'

'Carriage?' said Nicole.

'I don't think the lady came in a carriage, sir,' said Ponsonby.

'No? Well, look, we can't have you walking back all that way, Miss Nicholson. Ponsonby, can you arrange something? The landau, perhaps. And, really, someone ought to go with her.'

'Seymour, sir?' suggested Ponsonby. 'After all, I think he knows her.'

*　　*　　*

149

'You'd 'ave sorted it out, wouldn't you?' said Nicole confidently. 'If we'd been back in Whitechapel. You'd 'ave said, "Lay off, you little bastard!" and everything would 'ave been all right.'

She sat silent until they were about halfway down Pera Hill and then she said:

'It's 'Assan, see? I mean, 'e doesn't like it. It's a bit of a delicate subject. 'E doesn't like saz players. 'E said they're not really musicians and that they're nutters. And 'e doesn't like this one in particular because, well, look, it's a bit of a delicate subject –'

'Who is Hassan?'

''E plays the drums. And I've sort of paired up with 'im, like, and 'e doesn't like it when I – But I've told 'im there was nuffink in it. All it was, I took pity on 'im, see? I felt sorry for 'im, poor lost bleeding soul. That's all it was. Just bleeding pity. And 'e 'ad nice brown eyes.'

'The saz player, this is?'

'That's right. So, anyway I took 'im back to the flat once. Well, maybe more than once. But out of pity, that's all. That's all it was.

'But I made a mistake. I told that geezer about it.'

'Mukhtar?'

'Yes. 'Im. And then he wouldn't leave it alone. Kept asking me 'ow many times? When? "Christ, I don't know," I said. "I don't exactly keep a diary." But if 'e'd come to the flat, 'e said, 'e must have seen Lalagé. "No," I said, "we had this arrangement. She made herself scarce whenever I wanted to use the room. And I did the same for 'er." Of course, she didn't use it much. She'd got better places to go to.

''E said – this geezer – did she ever do a turn with 'im? "Look," I said, "I've *told* you. She wasn't interested in the likes of saz players." She'd got a bleeding Prince after 'er. She thought she was made. And 'e seemed crazy about 'er, there every night in the box, following 'er around like a little dog. She went off with 'im every night after the show. 'Ow she did it, I don't know, I mean, we were rehearsing all day and then onstage – And then she ran off with 'im and Christ knows what she was up to. I mean, to be fair, it wasn't all on 'is side, it was as much, at first, on 'ers.

'I tried to damp 'er down. "That sort of man is not for you," I said. "Oh, I don't know," she says. "It's not what you think," she says. "'E's interested in me as an artist." "Oh, yes," I say. "Yes," she says. "It's because I'm an actress. 'E's interested in the theatre, and –" "'E's interested in something else," I say. "That, too," she says, laughing. Well, there was no reasoning with 'er. Any more than there was with 'im. She was besotted with 'im and 'im with 'er.

'Anyway, I told the geezer all this but 'e kept coming back to the saz player. Did 'e come to the flat regularly, 'e asks? Well, fairly, I told 'im. For a bit. Not to see 'er, of course. Only 'Assan 'eard this and 'e wasn't too pleased.

'And did 'e bring his saz with 'im, asks the geezer? Well, I mean! I think 'e was more interested in another sort of instrument, I says cheekily. I don't think 'e understood, though. 'Owever, 'Assan did, and 'e wasn't too pleased at that, either.'

Nicole had to get back in time for the evening performance so Seymour took her to the theatre, leaving the landau, as Rice-Cholmondely had done, at the Galata Bridge. There was an atmosphere of tension about the theatre tonight.

'It's 'im,' said Nicole. ''E's got the 'ole place on the 'op.'

Mukhtar came down the steps at this point.

'Ah, there you are!' he said.

'I've been up at the Embassy,' said Nicole spiritedly. 'Looking after me rights!'

Mukhtar didn't seem quite to understand this.

'You'd better go in,' he said. 'They're waiting for you.'

Nicole scuttled in.

'What's all this about?' asked Seymour.

Mukhtar looked at him as if he'd come from another planet. Then he caught himself.

'Of course,' he said. 'You don't know!'

'Know what?'

'The saz player,' he said. 'He's disappeared.'

'I went to see him,' said Mukhtar. 'This morning, as arranged. But he wasn't there. I went to Mr Cubuklu's house first, as that was where we had arranged to meet. He goes there most mornings now to practise. But he wasn't there. He hadn't turned up this morning. So I went to his lodgings. He wasn't there, either. Nor were his things.

'Mr Cubuklu, I have to say, did not seem surprised. "They're very shy creatures," he said. I asked him if he knew where he might have gone, but he didn't. He just shrugged his shoulders. "Back to the mountains, I expect."

'I was not very pleased, and perhaps I showed it, for later in the morning he summoned me and showed me a letter which he claimed he had just received. It was from Babikr. He thanked him for all he had done for him but said that he was going away. That was all. He didn't say where he was going to. Just away.

'I have, of course, been trying to find him. I thought he might still be in the city. I know about his relations with that woman –' he gestured after Nicole – 'so I went round to her. She says that she's not seen him. I've tried the other people at the theatre but she was the only one who seems to have been able to make any kind of human contact with him.

'I thought he might have hidden in some corner of the theatre. There are lots of places where someone could hide. But I've spent the whole morning going through the theatre and I'm sure he's not there.

'So perhaps he *has* gone away. If he has he will be on foot and will not have got very far. I will alert my colleagues and I will find him.'

'Have you thought,' said Seymour, 'that he might be dead?'

Inside the theatre the band was striking up. It seemed to be a final rehearsal before the performance that evening.

Mukhtar hesitated.

'There is nothing else, I think, that I can do here. I have people out looking for him. Or for a body. Including down on the waterfront where perhaps he might have gone if – But there is somewhere else I need to go. Perhaps you would like to come with me? You might find it interesting.'

The heat had gone out of the sun. In a short while it would be dark but in that short space of time when it was still light and just pleasantly warm people were coming out of their houses. Women were doing their evening shopping, coming back with great baskets on their head or ringlets of bread around their arms. In the bazaars little groups of men were gathering to drink tea and talk.

Mukhtar led him past the bazaar area to a long street shaded with plane trees beneath which men were sitting at small tables writing. It was, said Mukhtar, the Street of Scribes. Here at this end they were copying books. They bent over the pages, with their reed pens and colour box, gold leaf pan and burnisher, filling the sheets with exquisite script or patiently giving the leaves gold bindings or decorating the covers in designs which had been determined before Byzantium fell.

They were copying books, whole books; yet not more than a quarter of a mile away, from the huge warehouses in the bazaar area, he could hear the heavy pounding of modern printing presses. It seemed astonishing that the two could coexist, the ancient and the modern, the new and the traditional. But that, he thought, was Istanbul, caught, at this point in time, uneasily between the two.

Further along the street the men at the tables gave way to humbler scribes who sat on the ground and wrote letters for ordinary people, who queued before them patiently awaiting their turn. It was to these scribes that Mukhtar went. He took a letter out of his pocket and went along the row showing it to each scribe. They all shook their heads but then one of them nodded and pointed further along the row. Mukhtar went to the scribe and squatted down beside him and they had a long conversation.

Then he came back to Seymour.

'This was the one who wrote the letter,' he said. 'He says that a man came to him this morning and asked him to write it for him. Babikr is, of course, illiterate and could not write himself.'

They began to walk back along the line of tables. On most of them now there was an oil lamp. Around each lamp was a halo of circling insects. Just beyond the edge of the halo the scribe worked obliviously on.

'But I am puzzled,' said Mukhtar. 'I asked the scribe to describe the person who wanted him to write the letter. And it was not Babikr.'

Chapter Eleven

'. . . forcing the Narrows.'

There was a little group around Chalmers and he had a map spread open on a table in front of him. The diplomats did not, however, seem very interested.

'Well, thank you very much, Chalmers,' said the Ambassador, beginning to get to his feet.

'Most interesting!' said Ponsonby, extricating himself from the group and heading hurriedly back inside.

'Yes, but, look –'

'Fascinating, old boy!' said Rice-Cholmondely, seizing the opportunity to rise from his chair.

The group broke up with remarkable speed. In a moment the military attaché was the only person left. He looked around and his eye fell on Seymour, peacefully sipping his coffee on the other side of the terrace. Swiftly scooping up his map and the small table, he brought them across and placed them in front of him.

'I know you'll be interested to see this, Seymour.'

Seymour was not so sure. However, he was wedged in by the table in front of him, the wall behind, and the eager Chalmers.

Chalmers smoothed the map out.

'Now, old boy, this is the Gallipoli Peninsula and here are the Dardanelles. And this is Gelibolu, the town, where I know you've been. Same word as Gallipoli, really, but for some reason most of the maps call the peninsula Gallipoli and the town Gelibolu. Now you can see at once the strategic significance of the Straits. Close them and no

Russian ships can get out of the Black Sea and no one else can get in. The Ottomans would control the whole show.

'And it would be easy to do. Just put a few guns here –' he pointed with his finger – 'at Kilid Bahr or Chanak Kale, or at Kum Kale and Sedd el Bahr, where the Straits are at their narrowest, and you've effectively done it. Lay a few mines, perhaps, and it's all wrapped up.'

'Mines?'

'That's right. Or, if you want, you could put guns here, at the other end of the Straits, just before it opens out into the Sea of Marmara. Here, say, just by the town of Gelibolu. No one could move. You would command,' said Chalmers triumphantly, 'the whole theatre.'

'Theatre?'

'Of war.'

'Oh, yes. Of course. Of course!' And then: 'War?'

'Got to be prepared for all eventualities, old boy. And I can tell you one thing: Johnny Turk is preparing, for sure.'

'Really?'

'He certainly is. Now, look, old boy, you can see at once the significance of this new road he's building. It goes right along the coast and it's to give access to possible gun emplacements at the far end of the peninsula. Here, say, at Sedd el Bahr. Or maybe at Gaba Tepe. Or even up at Suvla Point. If you've got a big show, you're going to need a lot of ammo and you've got to have a decent road behind you to supply it.'

'There certainly is a road being built, but –'

'The thing is, old boy, they're already starting to carry cement along the first part of it.'

'Cement?'

'That's right. To build the gun emplacements.'

'Oh, yes. Of course. But –'

'No doubt about it. That's what it's for.'

'Yes. I see.' A thought struck him. 'Then maybe Cunningham was right?'

'Cunningham? Right?'

'If he really was spying –'

'Now, look, old boy. I'm not saying he wasn't spying. That's just the sort of damned stupid thing he would do. Encroaching on other people's ground. People who know how to do it properly. But . . . *right*?'

'If that's what he was doing . . .'

'No, no. Look, old boy. Just look at the map. And bear in mind what I told you. Now, look, this is where he was landing. And where he was looking, presumably. Right in the middle of nowhere. Neither at Kilid Bahr nor at Kum Kale. Nor even at Gelibolu! He *couldn't* be right. Johnny Turk is not that daft. What he was up to there, I don't know, but he couldn't have been spying. Not if he had any brains at all. Well, maybe he hadn't got any brains and he *was* spying. But, really . . .'

'He might well have known about the road, though.'

'I don't know that the road's got that far yet.'

'Oh, yes, it has. Mukhtar has been pushing it along, apparently. The mudir at the local village said so.'

'Mukhtar? The terjiman?'

'That's right.'

'If I were you,' said the military attaché heavily, 'I'd watch my step as far as that man is concerned.'

'Really? Why?'

'He's got links,' said Chalmers mysteriously.

'Links?'

'With the army. He's in with a bunch of young officers. The Young Turks, they call them. They're a radical bunch, all for change. Revolution, in fact. Now we don't want that, do we? They think Turkey should be able to stand up for itself. Against the West, if necessary. That will be why he's pushing the road.'

'Well, I don't know about –'

'And holding back on Cunningham.'

'Holding back?'

'Well, he's the one who's supposed to be in charge of the investigation, isn't he? And he's not been doing too much investigation lately, has he? He's been over in Istanbul looking at something else. Ask yourself why, old chap. Ask yourself why.'

Seymour had already asked himself: and had come to a different answer. He thought it very unlikely that Mukhtar had relinquished the investigation. There was no doubt, however, that the focus of his investigation had shifted: away from the lonely beach near Gelibolu and to the Theatre of Desires. There it had become tangled up, or, at any rate, linked with the enquiry into Lalagé's death. And Seymour thought he could see why.

He was not sure, though, that he agreed with Mukhtar in his shift of focus. He thought there was still more to be found out at Gelibolu. And he thought he could see how to find it.

He intercepted Felicity as she came out for a break from the quartet's rehearsal.

'Would you mind? I know it's a long way.'

'If it would help,' said Felicity, 'I wouldn't mind that. And I'd like the sail. And I'd quite like to talk to the mudir's wife again. She's the one who would know about the soldiers.'

Then he went to see Chalmers. The attaché's eyes widened.

'Good God!' he said. 'Never thought of that! But, of course, you could be right. I'll get straight down there and nosey around. Give me a day or two. And the gun? Leave it to me, old chap. My sort of thing.'

Seymour went to Ponsonby to see if the attaché could be spared.

'Spared?' said Ponsonby. 'Only too readily!'

Then he went down to the theatre.

There was some sort of fracas at the foot of the steps. The band was gathered in the street and the drum player, evidently enraged, was trying to get up the steps. Higher up, just out of reach, the dancing boy lounged provocatively against the pillar. Between them, trying to keep them apart, was the agitated theatre manager.

'I'll kill him!' shouted the drum player, lunging.

The little manager somehow got in front of him and grabbed him.

'No! No! Think of the performance, please!'

'What performance?' asked the dancing boy, studying his beautifully painted nails. 'I don't think there will be one. Not if you're expecting me to go on.'

'Please! Please!' begged the little manager. 'Stop this! Both of you.'

'Let me get at him!' shouted the drum player, trying to push Rudi out of the way.

'Why don't you get rid of this dreadful man?' said the dancing boy, taking care to keep the manager between them. 'In fact, why don't you get rid of all of them? Let's not pretend that anyone comes here for the music.'

'Let's not pretend that anyone comes here to see *you*,' said the band's leader furiously. 'I don't know why you bother with him,' he said to the manager. 'He's nothing like as good as Lalagé was.'

'Nor Nicole!' said the drum player, shaking his fist.

'Oh, I don't know,' said the dancing boy airily, studying his nails again. 'I heard someone say how pleased they were to see a return to the old traditions. And not to have to watch some Western tart.'

He hastily stepped back to evade the drum player's lunge.

'Blind, were they?' said the kemengeh player.

'Deaf, too, I would think,' said another of the bandsmen.

'I'll have you know,' said the dancing boy, drawing himself up, 'that it was someone of importance.'

'Not that daft Prince of yours, was it?' said the band leader. 'If it was, I can tell you one thing, it's not your acting ability that he's interested in.'

'It's your backside!' shouted the drum player.

159

'Crude fellow!' observed the dancing boy. 'I don't know why you put up with him,' he said to Rudi.

'I don't know why we put up with you!'

'Because you have to,' said the dancing boy. 'Otherwise you wouldn't have a leading lady at all. You know,' he said to the little manager, 'I don't think I can go on this evening. I'm so exhausted from arguing with these louts. No, I really don't think I can.'

'You must! You must!' cried Rudi.

'No, I'm sorry, I don't think I can. You really must make up your mind, Rudi. Who can you do without? A bunch of two-a-penny hack musicians, or the one leading lady you've got left?'

'What about Nicole?' said the drum player angrily.

'Nicole?' said the dancing boy disdainfully. 'I thought we were talking about leading ladies?'

'Please! Please! Everyone! The performance! It must go on. Everyone must pull together. Ahmet –'

'Of course, I don't want to disappoint my admirers –'

'Of course you don't!' cried the manager eagerly.

'But then I don't know,' said the dancing boy, affecting to stifle a yawn. 'I'm so exhausted.'

'You must! You don't want to disappoint them, do you?'

'Of course, they are important people. Influential people.'

'That dopey Prince!'

'Not that dopey Prince, actually. Another one. Two of them. Two Princes,' said the dancing boy, savouring.

'Bollocks!' cried the band leader.

'And not just him. His friend, too. A most discriminating man! He says –' he scrutinized his nails again – 'that I am a sensitive interpreter of the old tradition.'

'Sensitive!'

'Think about it,' the dancing boy said to Rudi sweetly. 'Who can you best do without? This rabble? Or –' he coughed modestly – 'me?'

He retreated inside hastily as the drum player at last

managed to push past the little manager. Rudi dashed after them.

'Bastard!' they all shouted; to the air, unfortunately.

'What was all that about?' asked Seymour.

'He told Rudi to get rid of us. He said we were playing too loudly.'

'You *were* playing a bit loudly, Hassan,' said the leader.

'He was getting on my nerves. Poncing around on the stage like that! I'd had about as much of him as I could stand.'

'You should have beaten him instead, Hassan,' said the leader.

'Yes,' said the drum player thoughtfully. 'Yes, but, then, I didn't want to break a good drumstick. You don't happen to have a spare string, do you?' he said to the kemengeh player.

Rudi came back out and stood on the steps, mopping his brow.

'Actors!' he said. 'Or actresses. It's the same thing. They're more trouble than they're worth. If it's not on the stage, it's off the stage. They're either after someone or someone's after them! First, it was Lalagé. Now it's this little twerp. And we were doing so well, too! The first theatre in Istanbul, that's what we'd become. And now . . .!'

He buried his face in his hands.

'That, as a matter of fact,' said Seymour, 'is what I wanted to talk to you about. Can we go to your room?'

Rudi led him to his office, a small room in the complex of store rooms, props rooms and dressing rooms behind the stage. It was a dingy little room without a window but with tattered posters of the troupe on the walls, advertising not just their performances in Istanbul but also previous ones in Beirut, Damascus, Smyrna and some places Seymour had never heard of.

'Ah!' said Rudi, seeing Seymour looking at them. 'Those were the days!' He shook his head sadly: then, with one of those sudden turns of his, he switched immediately. 'Not that I regret coming to Istanbul. In some ways it was the making of us. The making! The first theatre in Istanbul! Never in my wildest dreams –! Well, perhaps in my very wildest! There we were one day playing to a few old men and the stray cats and dogs that had wandered in, and then the next, the whole of Istanbul was flocking to our door! Command performances –'

'Really?' said Seymour.

'Well, not quite,' Rudi admitted. 'But it would have come, it would have come. But royal patronage, certainly. And Palace interest.'

'Yes,' said Seymour, 'I wanted to ask you about that. I gather it even influenced your choice of material –'

'Not directly,' Rudi broke in. 'Not directly! I've always insisted on our freedom to put on exactly what we choose –'

'There was something described as "the Palace skit" which, I gather, you took off at the Palace's request –'

'Ah, that was out of courtesy. Purely out of courtesy.'

'And something you put in, or kept in, at the Palace's request. Something to do with the army.'

'Well, that was just, er, a good idea. Good advice. Always listen to good advice, that's my maxim. No matter where it comes from.'

'Even when it comes from the Palace?'

'That's right, yes. Yes, that's right.'

'So they were taking a close interest in what you did?'

'Oh, very close.'

'That's unusual, isn't it?'

'Unprecedented!'

'How did it come about?'

'Well, I suppose it was because of what we had become. When Cunningham first came along and showed us his

162

material, I didn't want to touch it. "Not our kind of thing," I said. "Too political." But he persuaded me to try it out. The odd sketch or two, you know. That was all it was at first. I thought, try it out, and then drop it if it doesn't work. But it did work! It worked amazingly. And soon the theatre was full! Every night! You see, no one else was doing anything like that. It was as if we were cocking a snook at authority, and that was something new in Istanbul. No one had dared do anything like that before. So, well, things took off.'

'You know,' said Seymour, 'what you say surprises me. You say you were cocking a snook at authority; and yet that the Palace supported you.'

'Not at first, not at first. We were definitely persona non grata. It was only when Prince Selim started coming.'

'He persuaded them?'

'No, no. No, no, no. It wasn't like that. What it was, was that he suddenly realized he could use us. You see, through his association with us he could be in the public eye, and in a way different from what he was normally and from the other Princes. It's no secret – I'm sure you know about it – that the old Sultan is on his deathbed and his successors are jostling for the throne. Well, Selim wanted to mark out a position different from the other parties in the jostle. They were traditional and conventional. He decided to be modern and improving. And what better way of showing this than associating himself with a theatre, *the* theatre, conspicuous for attacks on the old guard, the pashas, the people who'd been running the Empire for centuries? We were different, he was different; we were fashionable, he, suddenly, was fashionable, too.'

'But the Palace . . .'

'I think they were caught off guard. They hadn't realized the power of popular entertainment, they were only just getting round to the idea of the need for popular support at all. So Selim stole an advantage. And, naturally enough, the other Princes started doing something about it. And the Palace, too. If he can manipulate public opinion, they thought, so can we. And so they didn't close us down but started using us, too. Suggesting things. Of course we had to follow their suggestions. But that's how it was. It wasn't that Selim persuaded the Palace to take an interest in us, or at least, not directly. It was that they suddenly saw what he was up to and decided to take a hand themselves.'

'And this was all, in a way, thanks to Cunningham?'

'Well, I suppose you could say that. But you could also say that it was thanks to him that it all began to unravel!'

'How was that?'

'It was because of Lalagé. You know, just as I was saying. They cause more trouble than they're worth. But at first it helped Selim. You know, the Prince and the Actress! Well! They don't have actresses out here, you see, and people thought it was very advanced, very sophisticated. Just like Paris and Berlin! They were always going round together. And Lalagé really began to fancy herself. I don't know how she expected it to end. In her becoming a Princess?

'But, of course, while some people liked it and thought it was very advanced, others didn't. The fact she was an actress, for a start. They don't have actresses here, you see. They have a different attitude towards women.

'Go up the street, go just round the corner, and what will you find? I'll tell you: a snake-pit. And in the snake-pit there's a woman. On show. Nude, of course, and along with the snakes. That's how it is for a woman here. Or, at least, for a woman like Lalagé. An actress. Or it can be. Well, you take a look.'

'And you think that that was perhaps why Lalagé –'

'No, no, no. I'm not saying that,' said Rudi hurriedly. 'I don't know why she was killed, and I don't want to know. Don't get me wrong: I'm sorry about Lalagé. She was a good kid. And who's to blame her for fancying her chances with a Prince? It could happen. I've known it happen. And he seemed to be serious about her. Besotted with her, you might say.

'And we played along. We were glad to. We thought our

luck was in. A Prince! Royal patronage! Well, it makes a difference, you know. People listen to you if they think you've got someone big on your side. They don't push you around. So we were glad to play along.

'But then when Lalagé got killed everything went sour. There's a risk to being in the public eye. And suddenly everyone started thinking about that. We began to think that maybe we were wrong to tie ourselves too closely to Selim, or let him tie himself to us. Some people might not like it, people just as big as him. We began to get a tickle at the back of our necks. I don't hold with this talk about the Fleshmakers, I think it's all nonsense, but, you never know, there might be something in it. I mean, think of Lalagé.

'So when Selim pulled out, which he did after Lalagé's death, we were in a way quite relieved. It made it easier for us to shift our position a bit. Not stick our neck out quite so much. That boy's a twerp, Ahmet, I mean, but maybe he's got something. Maybe we ought to go back to the old ways? Just for a bit, anyway. I mean, if he's right, and there are people coming to see him . . .

'Do you think he's right? He could be. There's a Councillor been several times to see us, and a Prince. Prince Hafiz, who's just as big as Selim. And if they like him and like the old ways, well . . . In the theatre you've always got to stay close to your audience. I've always said that. So . . .

'Anyway, we've changed tack. Gone back to the old ways. That's why we're doing a lot of rehearsing at the moment. It's not easy. Everyone's got to change. The band . . .'

Seymour went to see the band after he had left Rudi. They were taking a break, one of the attendants told him, and could be found in the nearby park, the one he'd noticed on his first visit to the theatre.

And there they were, sprawled in the shade of the

bandstand, taking refreshment, as is the way of bandsmen the world over when they were not playing.

'It's the lips,' explained the flute player. 'You've got to keep them moist.'

'It's the fluid loss,' explained the drum player learnedly. 'When you're playing the drums, you sweat buckets. You've got to replace it.'

'It's the heat,' explained the kemengeh player. 'You wouldn't believe how hot it gets when you're playing down there in the pit. It really parches you up.'

'My God!' said Seymour. 'It's fortunate that I came when I did. You might have expired before I got here. Would it help if I ordered some beer from that stall over there? Or would your religious scruples . . .'

They were prepared, for the moment, to set aside their religious scruples. Seymour got one for himself, too, and sat down beside them.

'So,' he said, 'you're doing a lot of rehearsing? Would this be because of Rudi's new tack?'

The band leader shrugged.

'It's not that new,' he said.

'It doesn't make a lot of difference to you?'

'I play old,' said the drum player. 'I play new. I even play modern if they pay me enough.'

'You see, it's different here,' explained the leader. 'In Europe, or so they tell me, it's one thing or another. You go to a concert hall if you want classical, to a music hall or something like that if you want popular. But here it's not like that. Audiences are happy with both. In a place like ours you can play either. The tricky bit is fitting it to what goes on up on the stage. It doesn't matter what the music is as long as it goes with the performance.'

'We improvise,' said the kemengeh player.

'Isn't that difficult? I mean, how do you know what to play?'

'We sit in on rehearsals,' said the band leader, 'so that we can work it out.'

'We sort of fiddle around,' said the kemengeh player.

'And it takes shape,' said the flute player.

'We always know what we're going to do when we get to the actual performance,' said the leader. 'I mean, we don't just trust to luck.'

'So you're there for all rehearsals?' said Seymour, sipping his beer.

'That's right. Of course, we get paid for it.'

'Though not very much,' said the kemengeh player.

'Well, it sounds very difficult to me. Especially when it's a question of developing a new approach. But it's working out all right, is it?'

'We-e-ll . . .'

'Perhaps even better?'

'I wouldn't say that.'

'Better? With that twerp up front?'

'Ahmet? But I thought, from what he was saying, that he was a big hit?'

'I'd like to hit him, if that's what you mean,' said the drum player morosely.

'Apparently, people were coming to see him. Big people.'

'That Councillor the other night? But he didn't come to see Ahmet. Not the first time.'

'No? Who did he come to see, then?'

'That saz player.' The kemengeh player turned to the flute player. 'You know, you can say what you like, but that man could play! He wouldn't do for us, of course, he's not a band player. But he could play, all right. And he was the one that Councillor came to see. The Englishman brought him.'

'Well, thank you, Englishman! He brought the saz player in the first place, and that was a waste of time. And then he brought that dopey Prince, and see the trouble that caused! We'd be better off without him bringing people.'

'Anyway, I don't think the Councillor came just to see the saz player,' said the flute player. 'Because he came again, didn't he, after Babikr had left. Several times.'

'He definitely came to see Ahmet. He used to invite him up to his box. So he must have liked him.'

'I can't understand that,' said the kemengeh player. 'I can understand him coming to see that saz player, because, as I say, he could play. But that little twerp, Ahmet –'

'No talent at all. I'm surprised he couldn't see through him.'

'He even brought Prince Hafiz to see him.'

'Well, I can't understand that, either. I would have thought Prince Hafiz knew better than that. He's supposed to be a connoisseur, isn't he?'

'Maybe acting wasn't the particular talent that he was looking for!'

They all guffawed.

'I got that little bastard the other day, didn't I?' said the drum player, with satisfaction. 'He ponces up to the front of the stage and sort of pauses. You know, to make sure that everyone is listening to him. And then he opens his mouth. And then I hit my drum!'

'Couldn't hear a word,' said the flute player. 'Brilliant!'

'He opens his mouth again and I give it another roll!'

'He gets in a fury,' said the kemengeh player, laughing, 'and flounces off.'

'And little Rudi goes running after him. "Oh, please, Ahmet, come back! Do come back!" But he doesn't, not that time. Not at once, anyway.'

'And bloody good riddance!' said the drum player.

'Yes, but it was just as well it was only during a rehearsal,' said the band leader, 'and not during a performance. Rudi didn't like it.'

'He gave me a warning,' said the drum player. 'But I hope he's forgotten about it. Because that was the day there was all the trouble. You know, Lalagé. Well, I'm sorry about Lalagé but glad I got that little bastard.'

Seymour walked back with them to the theatre. They went inside and he walked on up the street. The street broadened out into a little triangle, and wedged against the apex of the triangle was a wire-mesh cage surrounded by a low wooden fence. You paid to go in and when you got there you could look down into a sunken pit. The pit was full of snakes. In the middle of the pit a woman was lying. She was completely naked and snakes were draped about and all over her. They lay in coils, rolls and bars, like richly decorated brocade mottled and inlaid with patterns in buff, orange and yellow. From time to time the woman stretched out a hand and touched the coils. Then there was a ripple of movement, a kind of liquefaction beneath the skins, as they all shifted. Then the movement subsided and the snakes went back to being as inert as they had been before and as she, apart from the touching out of a hand, had been throughout.

When Seymour got back to his hotel he found a note from Mukhtar. It said that Mr Demeyrel's report had now come through, and that the string that had killed Lalagé Kassim was indeed from a musical instrument: the saz.

Chapter Twelve

Seymour went to the theatre that evening. He managed to time his arrival for the start of the performance of Rudi's troupe. It was different from the performance he had seen before. Not only were some of the sketches different – the result, presumably, of Rudi's new tack – but, of course, there was no Lalagé. Nor, rather to his surprise, was Nicole there.

He was surprised at the difference Lalagé's absence made. He hadn't realized before how important she was to the troupe's performance, the way in which she gave them all a lead, the way in which they had all played off her. Tonight the troupe's dynamics were completely different. In Lalagé's absence, Ahmet queened the stage – in all manners of speaking – and they played off him. But somehow it didn't work so well. The interaction between the players was more clumsy, there was hesitation and uncertainty; and, of course, antipathy.

He realized suddenly, too, how important the music was. The band, too, played off the leading actor: only in this case it was playing, it must be deliberately, against him: slightly mistiming the cues, introducing unfortunate echoes, almost raspberries. He could see Ahmet getting cross.

But Ahmet himself was no help to anybody. He flounced around the stage stealing the limelight in a way which, if Seymour had been a member of the cast, would have thoroughly put his back up.

The audience, however, to his surprise, seemed to love

it. Were they, he wondered, such connoisseurs of guying that they could appreciate it even when actors guyed themselves? Or were they aficionados of the lost arts, relishing a return to old traditions which ignorant foreigners could not perceive?

When the troupe went off for a break Seymour leaned across the top of the box and asked one of the waiters to invite Ahmet to join him. 'Join an admirer,' was how he put it, and it worked.

Ahmet quickly appeared and accepted Seymour's compliments graciously. Seymour noticed that he drank the same green concoction as Lalagé had, and wondered if it was a special house lemonade charged to customers at the price of a souped-up champagne, but, on reflection, thought that possibly Ahmet was not well up in sophisticated drinking habits and had taken his cue from Lalagé.

He asked the dancing boy where he had learned his skills.

'Oh, Damascus and Beirut,' said Ahmet airily.

'I suppose,' said Seymour, 'that in something like this, while teaching goes a long way, natural talent goes further.'

'Just so,' said Ahmet, gratified.

'But, in the end, what is important is opportunity.'

'Exactly,' agreed the dancing boy.

'When it comes along, you have to seize it.'

'You certainly do.'

'But, then, I imagine, it won't come of its own accord. You have to make it for yourself.'

'That's also true.'

'You will remember, perhaps, that earlier in the week I saw you with Prince Selim on his estate. I imagine his support has been helpful to you.'

'The support of people like that is always welcome,' Ahmet murmured.

'Yes, I'm sure. The problem must be getting people like that to see you in the first place. You must have been very

171

pleased when Cunningham Effendi brought you to the Prince's attention.'

'Cunningham Effendi?'

'Wasn't it he who introduced the Prince to the theatre?'

'Yes, but –'

'I expect it was he who first pointed you out to him.'

'Cunningham Effendi?' said Ahmet, taken aback. 'But Cunningham Effendi didn't like me. He did everything he could to *stop* me from being recognized. "That little prick?" I heard him say once. "He doesn't act; he just strikes beautiful poses." It made me so angry. I could have spat. In fact, I did spit. On him. But that was when the Prince stepped in. "Now, now, Cunningham," he said, "he's a man of talent. I can see he's a man of genuine talent." So it was the *Prince* who spotted me. Not Cunningham Effendi.'

'I'm so sorry. So I've got it wrong. It was the Prince! All credit to him. Of course, when I met you with him, I could see how much he valued you.'

'Not at first. At first it was all that little bitch, Lalagé Kassim. He had become absolutely besotted with her. But she was already having an affair, with Cunningham Effendi. I don't think Cunningham Effendi minded at first, in fact, he rather encouraged Selim. But then he thought he was going too far and told him to back off.

'And the Prince flew into a terrible rage and said it wasn't for a Prince to back off, and he ordered Cunningham Effendi to keep away from her. Cunningham Effendi said he didn't take orders, and Prince Selim said, "In this country you do!" And they had an awful quarrel.

'And that little bitch, Lalagé, didn't know what to do. Which one should she go for? The Prince was, when all was said and done, a Prince; but, deep down, I think she preferred Cunningham Effendi. In the end she went for him, which was a mistake. The Prince was very offended and went off in a fury.

'He turned against her so much that Cunningham

Effendi had to do something about it. He tried to reason with him but Selim wouldn't even speak to him. So he tried other things. He even pushed me in the Prince's direction. "Catch him on the rebound," he said. But at first it didn't seem to work. He was still so angry about Lalagé. But gradually I brought him round. "You don't want to waste your time on that little bitch," I said, "when I can offer you so much more." And eventually he realized this and forgot about her.

'I would even have got him coming back to the theatre, you know, if I had had more time. Not that it mattered, because by then other people were taking an interest in me. Important people. Even more important than Selim. It was I who saved the theatre, you know.'

'Really?'

'There were really big people, and they were coming to see me. And the thing was, they really appreciated me. Not like Selim. Now I'm not saying anything against Selim. He's a friend of mine and I really value all he's doing for me. But he doesn't appreciate me in the way that they do. He doesn't really understand my talent. But they do. I could restore the whole tradition of the dancing boy. That's what they think.

'And that little fool, Rudi, never gives me credit. He'd be out of a job if it wasn't for me.'

'Certainly, the world now beats a path to your door. The discriminating world, at least, if what I hear is correct.'

'It is true that people of distinction are beginning to come,' said Ahmet, admiring his fingernails.

He returned, however, to his brooding.

'But Rudi doesn't appreciate that. He doesn't realize what I'm doing for him. Perhaps it would be better if he *did* go.'

'And a new manager was brought in?'

'Someone who understands talent.'

'Yourself, for instance?'

'Well,' said Ahmet modestly, but pleased.

*   *   *

173

Nicole was packing. She had her back turned to him and when she heard him come in, she jumped back against the wall.

'Christ!' she said. 'It's you, is it? For a moment I thought –'

'You weren't at the theatre tonight.'

'I'm getting out! It's too bloody 'ot for me!'

'Hotter,' said Seymour, 'than it was?'

She didn't answer him directly.

'Monique's getting out, too.'

'You're doing it together?'

'She's making 'er own arrangements,' she said evasively.

'What will you do?'

'I'm moving in with 'Assan,' she said, 'for the time being.' She shrugged. 'I'll look around. There's always work in some of the places.'

'Another theatre?'

'No,' she said. 'Not another theatre.'

'That's a pity,' said Seymour. 'I was at the performance tonight. They missed you. They're nothing like as good.'

She shrugged.

'Lalagé was better.'

'Why are you going now?'

'It's changing,' she said. 'There'll be no place for women.'

'Rudi's new tack?'

'I'm not blaming 'im,' she said. ''E's 'ad to do it. With the new lot moving in.'

'The new lot?'

'Well,' she said, 'you know the way it's been. First it was Selim. Now it's that new man, you know, the one who likes the old ways. And the old ways don't include women. Get out before you're pushed out. Or worse.'

'Like Lalagé?'

'Like Lalagé. I've been wondering why they picked 'er out. It's obvious, isn't it? She was the one who stood out. Stuck 'er neck out, you might say. Went round with 'im, with Selim. Drew attention to 'erself. I think 'e liked that. Maybe 'e even wanted it. And she liked it, too. "You silly bitch," I said. "It won't do you no good. They don't like that sort of thing out 'ere."'

She sat down on the bed.

'Well, I was right, wasn't I? She was the one they went for. And I reckon they meant it as a kind of warning.'

'Who to?'

'Selim, of course. And us. Telling us we were bloody disposable and should get out of the way. Women mean nothing to them. You seen that bloody snake-pit up the road?'

'What were they warning him about?'

'I don't know. Us, I suppose. To steer clear of us. Clear of the theatre, maybe. Lal said 'e was doing it deliberately. It was part of some game 'e was playing. 'E wanted people to see 'e was different. The thing was, it drew everybody's attention. Now they didn't like that. So I reckon they were warning 'im to back off. And Lal was the warning.

'Never been in a place before where it was like that. You know, where the theatre wasn't just a theatre, it was a bloody battleground. But that's what it 'ad become. And now Selim 'as pulled out and the other lot 'ave moved in.'

'Who are the other lot?'

'The ones who don't think like 'im, I suppose. The ones who want to go back to the old ways. But if the old ways include the Fleshmakers, you can count me out! So I'm going. And Monique is, too. If Lalagé was a warning, I'm taking it.'

'You were quite right!' said Chalmers, his voice indicating some surprise. 'There they were!'

He had returned from his expedition and had come at once to see Seymour.

'In the water?'

'No, no, back up on the beach. Tucked away under the

175

cliffs in a little lean-to. Locked, of course, but that was no problem. They were beginning to build a more substantial concrete block nearby, with a track leading down from the new road. Judging by the block's size it would take about twenty at a time. Of course, you wouldn't want too many. You'd have to put a guard on them. It would probably be just a temporary store where they'd keep them before shoving them into the water. When they needed to. I must say, it had never occurred to me. Smart of you, old boy, to think of that!'

'I asked myself why he needed to approach in the water.'

'Pretty cool! Suppose they'd been in the water? Of course, they wouldn't have been. Not yet. There's an international right of passage. But on the outbreak of hostilities, they could put them out in a moment. Phew!'

He shook his head.

'Who would have thought it? Mines!'

'Cunningham thought it.'

'I take my hat off to him. I've been following things pretty closely but I've not picked up the slightest hint. But he obviously had. Or perhaps he'd worked it out. And to think of him taking a look at it from the sea! Under cover of that mad swim of his! I must say, he pulled a fast one there. Tricked us all.'

'Not quite all. Someone shot him.'

'It wasn't an army gun, you know. I've been checking, as you asked. Not a standard army gun. Something lighter. Probably a sporting gun. You'd have to get it especially.'

'And there weren't soldiers there at the time,' said Seymour. 'Felicity's been checking.'

'So?'

'Somebody else, then. Which brings us back to the woman.'

'Woman?'

'The Hero.'

'Now, look, old boy –'

'There was a woman there. On that side.'

Chalmers looked troubled.

'Pretty good shot. For a woman.'

'They can shoot, you know.'

'Yes, but –'

He shook his head.

'Well, your business, not mine. I'll leave that to you. But the mines are certainly my business. I'll notify my people immediately.'

The troubled look returned.

'But suppose they know about it already? Suppose that bastard, Cunningham, has told them? I mean, it wouldn't be proper. Lines of reporting and all that. But that wouldn't have stopped Cunningham. All the same . . .'

'My guess is that they don't know about it. Not the people here, certainly. And my guess is, not the War Office, either. He wouldn't have told them. He wouldn't have *bothered* to have told them.'

'Then . . .?'

'Cunningham, you see, was cocky. He thought he knew it all. And he thought he could handle it all. Not just the mines but everything else out here. Better than the Ambassador.'

'Well, old boy . . .'

'I know. But he didn't know where to stop. Better than the Ambassador, yes, but also, I'm beginning to get the feeling, better than the Foreign Secretary back in London. Better than the Prime Minister, maybe. I don't think he believed in leaving it to his bosses. He knew better. He thought if he left it to them, they'd probably mess it up. So he decided to take care of it himself. As I say, he was a very cocky man; arrogant man, you might say.'

'Damned undisciplined, I would say,' said Chalmers. 'That's the trouble with those Foreign Office types, Cambridge and all that. They think they know everything. Can do anything, can get away with anything. But if everybody starts doing what they personally think is best, where will you be? There's got to be discipline. That's what I've always said. There's not been enough out here. The Old Man should have jumped on him. I've always said that.'

'Felicity,' said Seymour, 'did Cunningham think there was going to be a war?'

'Oh, yes,' said Felicity.

'What did he say about it?'

'He said it might not come for a year or two, but that it was bound to come. He would know it was coming, he said, and would tip me off. And then I was to get out at once and not muck about.

'I didn't believe him. It seemed so unlikely, somehow, I mean, when you look around you and you see everybody getting on with their ordinary lives, and all the chat and bubble in the markets, and everyone being so nice.

'I said that to Peter, and he said it was like being in a boat. There's all that sea beneath you and there's just a thin layer of wood or metal between you and it. And at the bottom there is a volcano which is one day going to erupt. Ordinary life is like the thin bit of metal. That's all there is between peace and war.'

'I think that's how diplomats think. It's the way they spoke to me at the Foreign Office before I came out here. I didn't believe them, either.'

'Why are you asking?' said Felicity.

Seymour hesitated.

'I think it's just possible,' he said, 'that Cunningham believed this and thought he might do something about it.'

Seymour went in search of Mukhtar and eventually found him: not at the theatre, where he suspected that he might be, and certainly not at Gelibolu, where he suspected he officially ought to be. Not even at the central police station, to which Seymour was sent by the police at the local station. But at the central barracks, which, in a way, figured. He looked up in surprise when Seymour came in and then jumped up from behind his desk and came towards him warmly.

'But how did you find me?'

'Oh, I sort of tracked you down. But I should have guessed.'

Mukhtar looked at him quickly.

'You might have guessed wrongly,' he said. 'I really am a terjiman. And I am really based at Gelibolu. But, as I think you have realized, yes, I do have contacts with the army. Unofficial ones, but, yes, strong ones.'

'You are a soldier?'

'I was a soldier. All young men are supposed to do a period in the army but, of course, a lot of them wriggle out of it. Especially the rich and more educated ones. Well, I had been to a law school and I think most people expected me to – but I didn't want to do that. I felt it was wrong to. An abuse of privilege. So I went in and served for several years. Then I decided to leave. They wanted me to stay but I felt I was being wasted. So I decided to become a terjiman.

'Well, once I had made it clear that I was going to do that, they decided to help me. The army is a powerful institution in the Ottoman Empire, Mr Seymour, and it usually gets what it wants. They secured me a posting to Gelibolu, where it was thought that I might be in a position to help them. The area, you see, is of some strategic importance. And, as the terjiman, I was able to push through some things they wanted done.'

'The new road, for instance?'

'Yes, the new road.'

'The mines?'

'Mines?'

'On the beach where Cunningham was to land. They're building a store. And a track down to it from the new road. They've got some there already.'

'So they have,' agreed Mukhtar, after a moment, watching Seymour warily, however.

Seymour waited.

'There is no reason why,' said Mukhtar, 'we should not put them there. We are a sovereign nation, you know. It is not as if they are in the water.'

'I think Cunningham may have wondered if some were in the water.'

'And so he swam across to see? Under cover of repeating Lord Byron's feat?'

'I think so, yes.'

'That would, of course, explain why he was swimming the wrong way.'

'Yes.'

'But, Mr Seymour, I am not sure you should be saying this to me. This was a very improper thing for Mr Cunningham to do.'

'Cunningham was a very improper man. May I say that I am not at all sure that his superiors out here know that that was what he was doing.'

'That I can believe,' said the terjiman drily.

'However,' said Seymour, 'the propriety of his action is no concern of mine. I am interested only in whether it contributed to his death.'

'And you think it might have?'

'I did think that at first, I must admit.'

'I can assure you, Mr Seymour, that it was not so. There are no soldiers there. If there had been, they would not have opened unprovoked fire on swimmers. The shot that killed Cunningham was not fired from a soldier's or a policeman's gun. Nor – if this is what you were thinking – was it fired by anyone in some secret organization or others in the employment of the Sultan. I can say this with assurance because I have gone into the possibility. It was my first thought, too.'

'But now you have changed your mind?'

'Yes.'

'You think that the explanation lies elsewhere?'

'Yes.'

'In Istanbul, perhaps?'

'Yes.'

'And so you have switched your enquiries.'

'That is so, yes.'

'Don't you think,' said Seymour, 'that we should lay our cards on the table?'

'Perhaps it would be better,' said Mukhtar, 'if we continued our discussion somewhere else.'

They left the heavy building with its corridors and sentries and went to a restaurant underneath one of the arches of an aqueduct. It was evidently a place favoured by soldiers for there were several sitting at the tables eating kebabs.

'They will not be able to understand us,' said Mukhtar quietly; but as an additional precaution he chose a table round the side of the arch. It looked out on a fruit market and all the time they were sitting there donkeys were going by laden with peaches and cherries, and porters, bent almost double, their hands hanging round their ankles, trudged past with box upon box of fruit roped in white towers on their backs.

'You switched your attention,' said Seymour, 'to the Theatre of Desires. Why was that?'

Mukhtar hesitated.

'Shall I tell you why I think that was?' said Seymour. 'You knew of Cunningham's involvement with the theatre. And that it had become the focus of political interest, with Prince Selim using it in his political campaigning. You knew that Cunningham had brought him to the theatre in the first place and you wondered how far Cunningham was involved in his campaigning. And if that had had anything to do with his death.'

'Go on,' said Mukhtar.

'But – I am guessing here – you couldn't see why it *should* have anything to do with his death. It would be an improper thing for him to do, yes, but, then, as we have agreed, Cunningham was an improper man. And he surely

181

wasn't important enough in Selim's campaign for anyone, on the other side, so to speak, whatever that was, to want to kill him. And why should Selim want to kill him when he was on his side? Helping him?'

Mukhtar nodded.

'I did wonder that, yes.'

'And then Lalagé Kassim was murdered. Was that nothing to do with it, something quite separate? A coincidence? Well, it could be. But I think you doubted it. At any rate, it was worth investigation.'

'It was worth investigation,' Mukhtar agreed.

'But how could it be? Now, I think you knew about how Cunningham was using Miss Kassim – as a spy, you would probably say, although I think myself it was probably just information-gathering, keeping an ear open for court gossip. But what I think you then began to suspect was that she might have picked up something, some item of information, that someone – it might even have been Selim himself – wouldn't have liked to get out. And to make sure it didn't get out they – whoever it was – decided to silence both Miss Kassim and Cunningham, since Cunningham would perhaps now possess the information.'

'My mind was running on those lines, yes.'

'You hinted as much to me. Yet I think you were not very satisfied with this argument, for all kinds of reasons.'

'Many reasons, yes,' agreed Mukhtar.

'But it would account for one thing: why Cunningham should have died in the way that he did. Because, you see, no one would connect it with any information that he had acquired at the theatre. Swimming the Dardanelles was a cover for him, but it was also a cover for whoever didn't want this information to get out. Someone saw a chance to use it.'

'That could be so, yes.'

'Now, I think,' said Seymour, 'it is you who have to carry on.'

The terjiman was silent for quite some time. Then he said:

182

'If I hesitate, it is not because I am unwilling to carry on: it is just that I am not quite sure how to. First, yes, the investigation had become a twin-track one, with both Cunningham and Miss Kassim. That might be a mistake, but the two were connected, very strongly. Their affair had been a very intense one. Deeper on his side than one would have thought, deeper, perhaps, than he at first intended, so that he was reluctant to relinquish her to Selim; and so deep on her side that in the end she rejected Selim.'

'I can throw something in here,' said Seymour. 'They went round together, Selim and Cunningham, as you know. But their relationship, though close, was also rather an odd one. Certainly with respect to sexual relationships. Someone suggested to me that it was as if Cunningham had to go first, as if Selim could only fall for a woman if Cunningham had tried her out first. Or perhaps it was simply that Selim was always to some extent dominated by Cunningham. But I think it happened again with Lalagé Kassim.'

Mukhtar nodded.

'It could well be. And it would add complication to the strange, three-way relationship. A relationship that was already complicated, since Miss Kassim was spying on Prince Selim and at Cunningham's instigation; although as I have said, Cunningham was on Selim's side. Perhaps, I asked myself, he was trying to bind Selim closer through use of this item of information that Miss Kassim had discovered, if there was such an item. If there was, incidentally, I have not found it. Yet.

'So, for the moment, I am concentrating on the other of my tracks. And here there is progress. You received my note about the saz string, yes? That, and the flight of the saz player, Babikr, says something, yes? Or so it would appear.

'But I am not sure that it is quite as it appears. Why would the saz player want to kill Miss Kassim? There was no relationship between them. She disdained him, he

183

appears, if anything, frightened of her. Hate? No, I find no hate. No motivation personal to him.

'I suspect, in fact, that he was merely an agent for someone else. And that brings me back to the theatre and its being a battleground for the rivals to the Sultan's succession. Selim was using it and rather successfully. Someone may have seen the need to – is this the right expression? – put a spoke in his wheel.

'Miss Kassim may have been the spoke. I am sorry to have to admit this, it does not reflect well on my country, but women do not count for much in our society. It will be different in the future, I hope. But at the moment a Lalagé Kassim counts for nothing. Someone may have decided to kill her as a signal to Selim, a warning to stop his theatre games. And they may have decided to use the saz player for that purpose.

'I do not know. But we shall see. For my colleagues have found the saz player out in the countryside and tomorrow they will be bringing him to me for questioning. And since I owe you something for the suggestion that put me on to him, perhaps you would like to be present? We shall turn over the card together, yes?'

Chapter Thirteen

There was a different feeling about the Embassy the next morning. Felicity, who was having a cup of coffee with Seymour, was tense; but so was everyone else. The diplomats went round with a preoccupied air. Servants, dressed in their best and with splendid red sashes, were everywhere, flicking with dusters at imaginary specks of dust. Cavasses strained to attention at every corner, while the Chief Dragoman darted around peering at them and everything to make sure all was in order.

The Ambassador, affecting confidence, announced that the quartet's rehearsal would go ahead as planned.

'Fiddling while Rome burns?' said Ponsonby, as they went past.

The sounds that came from the inner room where they were practising were far from assured and it was with relief, to them, evidently, as well as the audience, that they stopped after half an hour and came out on to the terrace.

Chalmers bustled around.

'Everyone ready?' he said. He glanced at his watch.

'For Christ's sake!' said Rice-Cholmondely. 'We're not going to synchronize watches, are we?'

'Well . . .'

A landau came in at the Embassy gates and drove up to the front of the Embassy. It contained a strikingly beautiful woman in a large hat and a flame-coloured gown.

The Chief Dragoman rushed forward and handed her down.

'Why, Iskander!' said Lady Sybil. 'How nice to see you again!'

The Ambassador came forward.

'Richard!' cried Lady Syb. 'How are you? It's been years!'

'Too many!' said the Ambassador. 'But you're still looking –'

Lady Sybil examined him critically.

'But you're not!' she said firmly. 'You've let yourself go. Or is it the bird-watching? John!' she cried, catching sight of Ponsonby. 'Where was it? Prague, or Vienna?'

'Vienna, I think,' said Ponsonby.

'And Alastair!' She gave her hand to Rice-Cholmondely. He bowed over it with old-fashioned courtesy.

She seemed to know everyone. Seymour was struck again by the smallness of the world of the English upper classes, where everyone knew each other, were probably related to each other, had perhaps been to school with each other, and had very possibly had affairs with each other.

Lady Sybil looked around.

'Where's my niece?' she said. 'They told me she would be here.'

Felicity, who had been lurking behind Seymour, came forward reluctantly.

'Hello, Aunt Syb,' she said.

'Darling!' They exchanged kisses. 'So this is where you've been hiding since you ran away!' She held her at arm's length. 'You look the better for it, I must say. Good colour. Is it the sunshine? Or are you having an affair?'

Felicity blushed.

'It's the sailing, I expect,' she muttered.

'Nonsense! There's a different look in your eye since I saw you last. And that is certainly nothing to do with sailing. Who is this young man?'

'This is Seymour,' said the Ambassador. 'He's a detective. Out from London to look into –'

'I know,' said Lady Sybil.

'Of course, of course. Sybil, I'm terribly sorry, we all are –'

'Yes, yes,' said Lady Sybil impatiently. She looked at Seymour. 'I shall want a word with you, young man,' she said.

'Of course.'

'I gather we are staying at the same hotel. Perhaps you will join me for dinner?'

'I would be delighted.'

'I was hoping, Sybil, that you might join us at the Embassy –' began the Ambassador diffidently.

'Tomorrow,' said Lady Sybil. She smiled at him. 'Thank you, dear. I look forward to it immensely. But perhaps you will show me around? I'd like to see how the place has changed since I was here last. And then, perhaps, we could come out here again for a drink? With John and Alastair and these other nice young men. Dinner at seven, sharp,' she said to Seymour. 'And, Felicity, I'd like to have a word with you, too. Perhaps you could come to the hotel before breakfast? I am always awake by five.'

'Oh, Lord!' said Felicity.

'Well, young man,' said Lady Sybil, over dinner that night, 'have you found out who it was that killed my nephew?'

'Yes,' said Seymour.

'Good!' Lady Sybil nodded approvingly. 'Rupert – he's the nephew that works at the Foreign Office, one of their rising stars, I always believe in working with rising stars, rather than those whose sun is setting, although, of course, it usually starts setting as soon as they reach the top, and I do believe in starting at the top – Rupert said that you were the man for the job. "Why?" I said. "Because he doesn't think like us," he said. "Well, that's a mercy," I said. "Foreign, is he?"' She looked at Seymour. 'You are foreign, aren't you?'

Seymour rose in rebellion.

'English,' he said firmly. 'Born and bred.'

'You look foreign,' said Lady Sybil doubtfully. 'The darkness, and something about the cheekbones. Central Europe, I would say. Hungary?'

'It is true,' said Seymour stiffly, 'that my mother was born in one of the Austro-Hungarian provinces.'

'And your father? One of the Seymours of Northumberland?'

'Actually,' said Seymour, 'he runs a timber business in the East End.'

'But the name . . .?'

Seymour was getting fed up with this social placing.

'. . . was adopted by my grandfather when he came to England. He was a Pole. His name was Pelczynski. He said that no Englishman would even be able to spell it, so changed it to Seymour.'

And put that in your pipe and smoke it, or the equivalent, thought Seymour.

Lady Sybil seemed, however, to have suddenly gone far away.

'Pelczynski?' she said. 'I knew someone of that name. A taxi driver. He used to drive a cab.'

'That's him,' said Seymour grimly.

'A tall, dashing, handsome man, who'd been an officer somewhere. In Russia, was it? And had had to escape because he was a Pole and they thought he was a revolutionary?'

'He *was* a revolutionary,' said Seymour.

'Stefan? Of course he was! It was very romantic. Thrilling, too! He used to tell me all about it. I was very young, then, just a girl, but . . . I knew him very well.'

Oh, no! thought Seymour. Not Grandfather, too!

'And you're his grandson?' Lady Sybil inspected him critically. 'Stefan was fair. You must take after your mother.'

'Yes, well . . .' said Seymour, anxious to move on, or, at any rate, away.

'Well, that is a relief!' said Lady Sybil. 'I've always said, we need to co-opt people from abroad. The English are so unimaginative. Take my family, for instance: thick as posts. So we've got to look outside our native stock. That's why we've got so many Scots in the Government. And Welsh, too. Although Lloyd George is not, it may surprise you to know, a man who knew me! And Winston, too; his mother was an American. And he certainly doesn't think like an ordinary Minister. Rupert was quite right. You're clearly the man for the job. As you've shown. For you found out who murdered Peter. And now you're going to arrest him.'

'I am afraid, Lady Cunningham, that it is not as easy as that.'

'No?'

'There is, for one thing, the question of what he was doing when he was shot. He was spying.'

'Well, of course.'

'You knew? But of course you did! He used to feed back his information through you.'

'Well, of course he did. He wanted to be sure that it reached the right people. And that meant not going through his superiors. Otherwise it would have just stuck on desks. You have no idea of the time it takes for anything to get through the system. And then, of course, they might have altered it. He wasn't having any of that! So, no, it had to go straight to the Prime Minster. I took care of that.'

'But, Lady Cunningham –'

'The trouble was, he didn't feed through all of his information. He kept some of it back. He didn't trust the Prime Minister, you see, to get it right, even when he did have the information. So he thought he'd better sort things out himself.'

'Yes, I do see that. And perhaps he told you what he had in mind?'

'It was something to do with the succession, I believe.'

'Yes. The present Sultan is ailing and his sons are jostling over who will take his place. Your nephew favoured a friend of his.'

'Well, of course! That is the thing to do. Go for the devil you know rather than someone you don't know, who is chosen by others and on whom, therefore, you can't rely.'

'I think your nephew had other reasons than that as well. For one thing, his candidate was quite Westernized and likely to favour the things that the Western powers wanted. To be fair, he stood for modernization and reform, too. But I suspect that the main reason in his favour was that your nephew thought he could influence him.'

'Well, that is, surely, very sensible of him.'

'I am not so sure, actually, that he was quite as influence-able as your nephew thought. However, he certainly did all he could to advance his interests. Perhaps he hoped that the Prime Minster would, too?'

'That was certainly the burden of the information that he wanted me to pass on.'

'But, you see, Lady Cunningham, to side with one inter-est is to run the risk of antagonizing others.'

'Well, of course.' There was a short pause, and then she said, 'And you believe that may have been the reason for his death?'

'Not quite. To do with the reason, perhaps. Lady Cun-ningham, we are in danger here of mixing in high politics and I do not share the confidence of your nephew that I can run the country better than those who have been elected to do so. I said that I knew who had killed your nephew. I think I do, but there are one or two things I need to confirm first. Tomorrow evening I should be in a posi-tion to enlighten you. I would suggest that we meet again for dinner but I know that the Embassy is hoping –'

'I will ask them to postpone it until the next day, when, perhaps, we shall all be in a position to celebrate.'

'Thank you. And I would like, if I may, to bring a friend with me tomorrow. He is the Ottoman official who has been handling the case.'

'Please do. I look forward to meeting him. You know,'

she said, as they rose from the table, 'you remind me so much of your grandfather.'

The saz player, Seymour noticed, had been brought not to a police station but to the military barracks at which he had met Mukhtar before. The barracks seemed to contain some cells, in one of which the saz player had been temporarily lodged. It was at the end of a long corridor and, Seymour, thought, probably underground. It was completely bare and the saz player was sitting bowed on the ground.

'You must come with me,' said Mukhtar, and took him to another room, which was furnished sparingly with a table and two chairs, one on either side of the table. Mukhtar summoned another chair and they sat down, the saz player, Babikr, on one side of the table, Mukhtar and Seymour on the other side.

'Babikr,' said Mukhtar softly, 'you need not fear, but you must answer my questions.'

The saz player nodded. He had been allowed to keep his saz and now it stood beside him on the floor. From time to time his hand reached down to touch it, as if he needed its reassurance. He was dressed in an old white galabeeyah and had a beaded skull cap on his head. Apart from a first, agonized look at the terjiman he kept his eyes fixed on the table.

'Babikr,' said Mukhtar, 'why did you run away?'

The saz player moistened his lips, as if he was about to speak, but then shook his head mutely.

'Were you frightened?'

Babikr nodded, but kept his eyes on the table.

'Who were you frightened of?'

The saz player said nothing but made a gesture of despair. Seymour guessed that he had been frightened of just about everything and everybody: the big city, the fluent people, the hostile band, even, perhaps, those who had befriended him. In picking him off the street Cunningham had done him no service.

'Perhaps you were frightened of me?' suggested Mukhtar. 'Perhaps Mr Cubuklu told you that I wanted to talk to you?'

After a moment, Babikr nodded.

'Perhaps Mr Cubuklu could see that you were frightened, and said that you didn't need to see me if you didn't want to, you could run away?'

In Whitechapel, thought Seymour, there may be objections to the questions, but here in Istanbul, given the nature of the man, he could see you wouldn't get far if you tried anything different. Certainly it produced a response: Babikr nodded.

'I expect he said he would help you. Did he tell you where to go? No? Just that you should go at once? And did he suggest that you should send him a letter telling him what you were doing? No?'

Letter? The saz player looked aghast at the thought.

He shook his head vigorously.

'Good. Now I have a question on something else. Mr Cubuklu asked you to play for him, yes? And to play before all the people. Yes?'

The memory alone seemed to make the saz player wretched.

'I expect you found it very hard to play before the people like that. It was not the way you usually played, was it? Not in a rich room and before rich people.'

Babikr shook his head vigorously.

'But you did it because he asked you, and had been kind to you. Did he ask you to do anything else for him?'

The saz player was locked in immobility.

'I think he did, Babikr, and I want you to tell me what it was.'

Babikr opened his mouth as if he was going to speak, but then could not.

'I think he asked you to do something that shocked you.'

Babikr said nothing.

'Something which made you very unhappy.'

Mukhtar waited, but the saz player didn't, perhaps couldn't reply.

'Babikr, this is something which you must tell me.'

He waited again, but the saz player seemed able only to look at the table in misery.

'Let me try to help you. I want to help you, Babikr. At the theatre, the theatre where you worked, there was a woman.'

Unexpectedly, this produced a response.

'Two,' muttered Babikr.

'Two women? Ah, yes. One was kind to you, wasn't she? when the band was being unkind. The other – well, she was not kind to you, was she?'

Babikr shook his head.

'Not kind. Did you hate her for that?'

Babikr looked startled.

'Hate?'

Seymour had the impression that the saz player had never in his life hated anybody, that it was, in a sense, too bold a thing for him to do.

'No?' said Mukhtar. 'Well, perhaps that was a pity. For it would have made it easier for you to do the thing that Mr Cubuklu asked you to do.'

And now Babikr really did seem paralysed. For a long time he sat there just gazing at the terjiman.

'God knows all,' he said at last, hoarsely.

'Well, of course, he does. He sees all and knows all. Remember that, Babikr, for it means that even if you say nothing, what is known, is known. So I ask you again: what was it that Mr Cubuklu asked you to do?'

Babikr's face began to work.

'God sees all and knows all. He knows what you did. But if it was at another's bidding, then that counts for you. Did Mr Cubuklu ask you to do something to Miss Kassim?'

'Yes,' whispered Babikr.

'To take one of your strings?'

'Yes.'

'And take it to Miss Kassim?'

'Yes.'

'And kill her?'

'Yes.'

Mukhtar sat back.

'It is hard for you, Babikr, I know. But it was right that you should tell me. For killing Miss Kassim was a terrible thing.'

'But I did not kill her!' burst out the saz player, weeping.

'But –' began Mukhtar.

'He asked me, but – but I said I could not.'

And now, suddenly, the saz player became voluble.

'I said I could not. I could not do such a thing. And then he was hard with me, and said that I must do it. That he had done much for me and could do more. That what he was asking was nothing. That she was nothing and had sinned in the sight of God, that it was right she should be punished. And I said that might be so, but that I was not the man to punish her. And then he became angry with me and spoke to me bitterly and said who was I to set up any judgement against those of my betters? But still I would not.

'Then he railed against me and said he was very displeased with me. But still I would not. Then, at last, he left it, saying that if I would not do it, there were others that would, and that they would wax rich, and that I would not. But I did not mind that, for I knew in my heart that what he was bidding me was wrong, that although she was but a woman, even a woman has a place in God's sight.

'And so we left it. But before we parted he told me to give him one of my saz strings. I was puzzled, because I knew he had no saz of his own. Nevertheless, I did as he asked. But afterwards, when I heard about Miss Kassim, I was troubled, and asked myself if what I had done had made for her death. And I could not acquit myself completely. So when he suggested that I go, I went with relief.'

'Well!' said Mukhtar, after a moment. 'You have spoken, and what you have spoken, you have spoken. Will you swear to it?'

'I will swear,' said Babikr.

After the saz player had been taken back to his cell, Seymour returned with Mukhtar to his room. The terjiman ordered coffee and they sat for a while in silence.

Then Mukhtar seemed to shake himself.

'Well,' he said, 'it is not quite as I expected. But, clearly, now, I must go and see Mr Cubuklu. I wish I had more, though, to go and see him with. It will be his word against Babikr's. A Councillor's against a saz player!'

He shook his head gloomily.

'Perhaps I can help,' said Seymour.

The little theatre manager received them uneasily.

'It goes on,' he said, distressed: 'this terrible thing!'

'It will not go on much longer.'

'Of course, anything I can do . . .'

'Well, yes,' said Seymour. 'And first I would like you to cast your mind back to the day Lalagé was murdered.'

'A terrible day!'

'Which went wrong for all kinds of reasons. The band was playing up. The drummer –'

A look of anguish passed over Rudi's face.

'The drummer?' he said.

'– blew what in England we would call a musical raspberry.'

'In Vienna we call it a musical fart.'

'Very off-putting! And it wasn't the only thing. There

195

was considerable antagonism between the band and Ahmet and things were very difficult that day. They reached such a pitch that in the end Ahmet flounced off in a towering rage.'

'Terrible!' moaned Rudi. 'Terrible! But not unusual.'

'But, of course, it disrupted rehearsals. You went after him to bring him back.'

'As one was always having to do. The life,' said Rudi, 'of a theatre manager is sometimes quite impossible!'

'You remember going after him?'

'Oh, yes.'

'Did you catch up with him?'

'Yes.'

'And then what happened?.

'What happened?' Rudi passed a hand over his brow. 'Well, I argued with him. Pleaded with him. Abased myself, you could say, which is what he liked. It usually works. But not this time. He was screaming, positively *screaming*, with fury. I could get no sense out of him.'

'And in the end?'

Rudi shrugged.

'Left him. Left him to cool down. That usually works, too, if nothing else does. It worked on this occasion. Eventually. Only after a long time, though.'

'But then he came back?'

'Yes.'

'And you carried on?'

'Yes, but only until Lalagé – She had gone off, you see, to change her costume. But then she didn't come back. I sent someone, Monique, I think, to kick her up the ass – I'd had about enough of actors' tantrums by then. And then Monique came back and said – Oh, my God!' said Rudi. 'It was terrible!'

'And at this time,' said Seymour, 'Ahmet was back with you?'

'Yes.'

'But previously he had not been with you. When you left

196

him, after failing to persuade him to come back, where was he?'

'Where was he?'

'When you caught up with him.'

'On his way back to the dressing rooms.'

'You are sure about that?'

'Yes. I went with him. I was trying to persuade him.'

'And where did you leave him?'

'At the end of the corridor. The one the dressing rooms were in. I realized it was useless to go on. He was hysterical. He took off his tunic and threw it on the floor. He said that this was the last straw, that he had had enough, that he was leaving the theatre and would never come back. He has said things like that before, it's best just to leave him to cool down –'

'And when you last saw him he was going along the corridor?'

'Yes, he took off his costume. It was all an act, of course, he wouldn't really –'

'The dressing rooms?'

'Yes, he was in costume, and – My God!' whispered Rudi. 'The dressing rooms!'

'Ahmet,' said Mukhtar, 'do you recognize this?'

'No,' said Ahmet. 'What is it?'

'It is a saz string,' said Mukhtar. 'Like the one you used on Lalagé Kassim.'

The dancing boy lost colour.

'You do not know that!' he said. 'You cannot know that!'

'She was alone in the dressing room,' said Mukhtar. 'You knew she would be there. Alone. When did the idea occur to you, Ahmet? As you rushed from the stage in anger? When your heart was full of rage and spite and you wanted to strike at someone? Or was it earlier? Had the idea already been there? Been put there, perhaps? And you

197

were merely biding the opportunity? Which was it, Ahmet? This is important.'

'Neither!' said Ahmet. 'Neither!'

'Shall I tell you which I think it was? I think the idea had been there before. Planted in you. And that when you were onstage and you saw Lalagé walk off to change, you thought, this is my chance! She will be alone, and everyone else is here and will not interrupt us.'

'This is nonsense!'

'And do you know why I think the idea was there before? Because of the saz string. You would not have had a thing like that with you unless it had been planned before.'

'I know nothing about a saz string. Why don't you ask Babikr, the saz player?'

'I have. And he says he gave a saz string to someone. And that someone, I think, passed it on to you.'

'A saz string? What is a saz string?'

'Something that is not exactly common. And so it can be traced.'

'Look to the man with the saz, then, and not to me!'

'But you were there, Ahmet, and he was not.'

'Who says I was there?'

'Rudi. He came with you almost to the door. And then he parted from you. She was there and you were there. The two of you. Alone.'

'How do you know that? It could be anyone. Anyone could have been up there!'

'Ah, but no, they couldn't. The rehearsal was going on, remember. Everyone was onstage. Or in their appointed place. I know. I have checked.'

'Someone could have come in off the street –'

'But Abdul, the porter, sits at the door, and he swears that no one came in. You were the only person there at the time, Ahmet. At the same time as Miss Kassim. And so I ask you again, Ahmet, who put the idea in your head? And gave you the saz string?'

Chapter Fourteen

'But I still don't see,' said Lady Cunningham, 'what all this had to do with the murder of my nephew.'

They were sitting at what Seymour reckoned must be the best table in the hotel's restaurant. It looked out over green grounds and then down at the blue waters of the Bosphorus; and then, beyond that, to the woody glades where Prince Selim had his estate. The sun had just gone down and the sky was still flame-coloured, and in places the blue of the water had become coppery red.

Lady C. believed in dining well. There was a different bottle for every course, several courses, and an array of glasses. Mukhtar, with a Muslim's strictness on alcohol, was not drinking; so Seymour felt a certain compulsion to see that Lady Cunningham's bounty was not wasted. He rather wished that he had suggested that Felicity should be there, too, and had even mentioned as much to her. Felicity, however, still recovering from her early breakfast with her aunt, had firmly turned the hint down.

'Well, let me outline the connection,' said Seymour. 'You will remember that your nephew originally set out to replicate Leander's feat of swimming the Dardanelles.'

'Yes, but he didn't,' said Lady Cunningham. 'He swam the wrong way.'

'I think he originally intended to swim it the right way, from Abydos to Sestos, but then he learned about the possibility of there being mines on the Abydos side and decided to make a switch so that he could take a look under cover of the swim.'

'That would have appealed to him,' said Lady Cunningham. 'He always believed that traditions could be improved.'

'Just so. What it meant, though, was that his Hero had now to be on the other side. When he had first thought about it, he had envisaged Hero as being in her true place on the Sestos side and had, indeed, when he was still thinking of Felicity as a possible Hero, placed her there. But then, for some reason, he changed his mind.'

'He probably thought,' said Lady C., 'that Felicity *couldn't* be his Hero because she was his cousin. In some ways Peter was surprisingly strait-laced.'

'But having a Hero had always been part of his intention; so I was surprised when on the actual day she was missing. Only she wasn't missing.'

'But I thought –' began Lady C.

'In the initial reports there was no mention of a woman waiting for him. Mohammed, the boatman, had not seen one, and by the time the kaimakam had arrived, the woman had gone. But she had definitely been there. My colleague, here, had learned as much from some small boys. And I confirmed it myself. So the question was, what had happened to her?

'With the aid of your niece, Lady Cunningham –'

'Felicity? What has come over the girl? She used to be such a pudding!'

'– I learned that someone had been picked up from the Abydos side after the shooting. Only that person was not a woman.'

'Then –'

'It was a man. And a man had, actually, been put ashore in the cove earlier, before the shooting. A man. However, there was one interesting thing that I had learned from the small boys and that was that when they had seen the woman, after the shooting, she had been taking off her clothes.'

'Really?!' said Lady Cunningham, surprised, a little shocked, and rather entertained.

'I had heard that, too,' said Mukhtar. 'But I had dismissed it as the smutty talk of little boys.'

'But it turned out to be crucial,' said Seymour. 'For it meant that the Hero was not a woman but a man. The fiction that Leander was swimming across to a woman was maintained. I have a feeling that your nephew quite enjoyed playing with the legend in this way. But, of course, it also meant that after the event it was particularly difficult to track Hero down.

'And this was important, for, you see, if, as appears to have been the case, the Hero was the only person present when your nephew landed, then he was the only person who could have killed him.

'Now, once one accepts that the Hero was actually a man dressed up in woman's clothes, some questions immediately suggest themselves. What sort of man? And one answer could be a man who was used to dressing up as a woman, a man who quite liked dressing up as a woman. And there was one man that Cunningham knew who fell strongly into this category, an actor at the theatre he frequented. Now, we know that in his search for a Hero, he had asked various actresses at the theatre if they would take on the role, but they had refused. Might he not have gone on to ask the actor? I think that would have quite appealed to him, too. And it would certainly have appealed to the actor, and for a number of reasons, which I will come on to.

'You will have guessed that I am talking about Ahmet, the dancing boy, the person who also murdered Lalagé Kassim. And there is your connection, Lady Cunningham, the one you asked for: the person who murdered Miss Kassim also murdered your nephew. He was waiting for him when he landed; and he killed him with a single shot. It was a very good shot. But, then, Ahmet *was* a good shot. I have seen him shooting, myself. He was very keen on shooting. He even had ambitions to go into the army.'

Mukhtar stirred restlessly.

'He may have had ambitions,' he said, 'but I can assure

you that the army does not make up its ranks from dancing boys.'

'Ah! But he hoped it would. And he had someone who
had influence and would speak up for him with the army.
And who was prepared to do that if Ahmet would do what
he asked him.'

Seymour looked at Lady Cunningham.

'Your nephew, Lady Cunningham, had made friends in
high places. In particular, he had a very intense relationship with one of the Sultan's sons. He knew, of course,
about your nephew's plan to swim the Dardanelles.
Indeed, he offered to help him. He took him and the small
rowing boat that was to accompany him to the starting
place. The plan was that he would pick him up from the
other side when he had completed his crossing.

'Unknown to your nephew, though, his felucca had
already sailed to the proposed landing place earlier that
morning and had put ashore the man who was to kill him.
He did indeed cross to the landing place that evening but
it was to make sure that the killing had taken place. Then,
from another point, he picked up the killer and took him
back to Istanbul.

'While your nephew was swimming across he returned
to the other side. In fact, he walked to the nearest town and
had his hair cut. This puzzled me: why would a Prince go
to a bazaar barber to have his hair cut? It didn't seem at all
likely. Then I realized: it was to establish his presence on
that side of the Straits at the critical time. If anyone asked
about his connection with your nephew's death, he had an
independent alibi.'

'But why,' said Lady Cunningham, 'would he want to
kill Peter? They were friends, were they not? A particularly
intense relationship, I think you said?'

'Yes. And reinforced by the fact that your nephew
believed that he could establish Selim as the next Sultan
and so, under his guidance, make sure that the Ottomans

202

were on the British side when the war that he was sure would come, did come. In that way, he thought he might even stop it happening. But his plans came apart precisely because of the intensity of their relationship – that, and its peculiarity.

'Someone told me – a lady herself, actually – that, as I gather is sometimes the aristocratic way, they even shared girlfriends. But she added something that I found intriguing, that while the Prince seemed unable to take the first step in a relationship himself – he needed your nephew to do it first – once he had committed himself, he felt peculiarly strongly about it. He became what my informant described as almost insanely jealous. And also extremely uncertain, for, describing her own experience, she said he appeared to be jealous of both the woman concerned *and* your nephew.

'The same pattern was repeated when your nephew introduced him at the Theatre of Desires. He was attracted to Miss Kassim, with whom your nephew was already having an affair. I don't think your nephew minded at first but then as the relationship between the Prince and Miss Kassim gained in intensity he tried to get the Prince to step back.

'He had initially encouraged her in the relationship in the hope that she would pick up court information which would be useful to him. But when he saw how the relationship was developing he became uneasy. He had seen, on the occasion that I previously mentioned, the Prince's behaviour become increasingly unstable and, indeed, violent and he feared that the same thing was happening in Miss Kassim's case.

'He tried to put an end to the relationship but it had gone too far. The Prince refused to back off. Indeed, he insisted that it should be your nephew who backed off. Your nephew refused, and the two quarrelled violently. Now normally your nephew was able to sort this out and resume the friendship, but on this occasion he couldn't. The Prince did, indeed, back off but his friendship for your

203

nephew had turned to hatred. So much so that in his rage he needed to kill him.

'The tool was already to hand. He had previously made the acquaintance of the dancing boy. Again, ironically, your nephew had encouraged this. But the Prince had discovered things about Ahmet that your nephew had not: his ambition to join the army. The fact that he was an unusually good shot, his stupid vanity and his intense jealousy. All this and the Prince's superior social position made it easy for him to persuade Ahmet to kill your nephew.'

'So,' said Lady Cunningham, 'if I have followed you correctly, Ahmet, the dancing boy, murdered both my nephew and Miss Kassim: but in the one case at the instigation of Prince Selim and in the other case at the instigation of . . .'

'Mr Cubuklu, who was acting on behalf of Prince Hafiz and trying to thwart Selim's attempt to present himself as a progressive and a modernizer. May I say that I think Mr Cubuklu also saw himself as acting on behalf of conservative court circles who were shocked at Selim's open flirtation with a woman they regarded as totally unsuitable.'

'I take it that you have already taken steps?'

'Ahmet is in custody,' said Mukhtar.

'And Prince Selim? And Mr Cubuklu? Not to mention Prince Hafiz?'

'Well . . .' said Seymour.

'It is not quite so simple,' said Mukhtar. 'Who will believe the word of a dancing boy against the word of a Prince? Or a Councillor?'

'So they will escape scot-free?' said Lady Cunningham. 'I must say, I find that unacceptable.'

'Naturally I shall do my best,' said Mukhtar unhappily. 'But I am just a terjiman.'

Lady Cunningham was lost in thought.

'I do, as a matter of fact, have some contacts in court

circles here,' she said. 'My old friend, Bebek, for instance. Perhaps . . .'

'Bebek?' said Seymour.

'This unfortunate attack on your nephew's boatman?' Bebek Effendi sighed. 'Over-zealous subordinates, I'm afraid. Of course, he would have come to no harm. The intention was just to frighten him off. I won't conceal, my dear Lady Cunningham, that some of us have an interest in Prince Selim. An imperfect instrument, I agree, and perhaps our interest is waning. But he seemed the best hope among the potential successors and so it seemed advisable to protect him. Naturally, our protection would not have extended so far as to try to cover up murder. And certainly not the murder of your nephew, Lady Cunningham, which I deeply regret. All we had in mind was concealing Prince Selim's interest in what seemed to us the bizarre episode of your nephew's attempt to swim the Dardanelles.'

They were sitting in one of the inner rooms of the Palace; Lady Cunningham on a low divan, Bebek on a chair beside her, and Seymour and Mukhtar on low stools.

'Not his killing?' said Seymour.

'Killing? Of course not! How could you think such a thing?'

Lady Cunningham's face, however, was cold.

'And does your protection extend to him now?' she said.

'Well . . .'

'I would regard that as very unsatisfactory,' said Lady Cunningham.

'Our interest in him has certainly waned,' said Bebek. 'We no longer think – I believe I can say this – that he is the man to fulfil our hopes. We shall be looking elsewhere. Is not that punishment enough?'

'No,' said Lady Cunningham.

Bebek sighed.

'I understand how you feel, my dear Lady Cunningham. And if it were left to me he would now be at the bottom of the Bosphorus in a sack. As used to happen in the days of the Sultan's predecessors. Or in the days of his devoted servants, the so useful Fleshmakers. But in these degenerate modern days we have to proceed more circumspectly. Make use of courts of law and such things, where, unfortunately, one can never be sure that the right result will be obtained. Particularly in the case of a member of the Sultan's family. And so, my dear Lady, we have to express our disapproval in other ways. But I can assure you, the disappointment of his hopes will be a severe blow to him.'

Not severe enough, Lady Cunningham clearly felt.

'I reserve my position,' she said.

'Bebek Effendi,' said Seymour, 'I wonder if you could explain one thing to me: does Mr Cubuklu share your views on the Fleshmakers?'

'He certainly pines for the good old days,' said Bebek.

'I wondered about the saz string, you see. Why did he choose that way particularly for her to die?'

'He has always been a conservative man,' said Bebek.

The thought, though, had put something else into his head.

'I would not wish to equate the loss of your nephew, Lady Cunningham, with the loss of someone such as Miss Kassim, but, with your extravagant passion for justice, you may feel that Mr Cubuklu is getting less than his due deserts. I think I can promise you that his days at court are numbered: and that he will in future pursue his enthusiasm for the old through the contemplation of rocks in the stony wastes of Outer Anatolia.'

Seymour decided to spend the evening pursuing Felicity.

Lady Cunningham, unusually silent, retired to her room, deep in thought.

*   *   *

She emerged the next morning her usual self.

'I have decided,' she announced at breakfast, 'that I shall go on safari in Africa, and I have invited Prince Selim, as a former friend of Peter, to come with me.'

'Is this a good idea, Aunt Syb?' said Felicity uneasily.

'Certainly, my dear. I am an expert shot.'

'Well, Seymour,' said the Ambassador, 'I suppose this means that you will be leaving us?'

'I'm afraid so, sir.'

'A pity. I do feel that the shearwater on that part of the coast need studying.'

'Absolutely right, sir!' said Chalmers eagerly. 'In fact, I was rather intending to take an interest in the birds myself. I was hoping, sir, that you would share some of your great knowledge with me.'

'Glad to, Chalmers, glad to,' said the Old Man, much gratified.

'Now, how was it that they nested, sir? On one leg, was it?'

'Well, nice to have met you, Seymour,' said Ponsonby, shaking hands. 'I gather from Lady Cunningham that you know Rupert.'

'Rupert?'

'A nephew of hers. Works in the Foreign Office.'

'Oh, yes. Yes. A little.'

'I daresay that means we may be seeing more of you.'

'Why don't you pop over for the weekend sometime, old boy?' said Rice-Cholmondely. 'The Oriental Express is very handy. Goes direct to Istanbul. And then we could go to the theatre.'

'Do you think they need an Arabic interpreter in White-chapel?' asked Felicity, lying beside him.

'Not yet,' said Seymour, 'but, the way things are going, they probably will.'

Mukhtar said that he was being transferred to a more central post in Istanbul. He was leaving Gelibolu: Gallipoli, as it became known to the world four years later, in 1915, when Chalmers' mad visions were translated into reality and the Dardanelles became an Armageddon; and the real Fleshmakers took over.